Lock Down Publications and Ca$h Presents

Secure Da Bag

The Price of Loyalty

Written By

IRA B.

Copyright © 2026 IRA B.
SECURE DA BAG

All rights reserved. No part of this book may be reproduced in any form or by electronic or mechanical means, including information storage and retrieval systems without permission in writing from the publisher, except by a reviewer who may quote brief passages in review.

First Edition 2026

Printed in the United States of America

This is a work of fiction. Names, characters, places, and incidents either are products of the author's imagination or are used fictitiously. Any similarity to actual events or locales or persons, living or dead, is entirely coincidental.

Lock Down Publications
P.O. Box 944
Stockbridge, GA 30281
www.lockdownpublications.com

Like our page on Facebook: Lock Down Publications
www.facebook.com/lockdownpublications.ldp

Stay Connected with Us!

Text **LOCKDOWN** to 22828 to stay up-to-date with new releases, sneak peaks, contests and more…

Like our page on Facebook:
Lock Down Publications

Join Lock Down Publications/The New Era Reading Group

Visit our website:
www.lockdownpublications.com

Follow us on Instagram:
Lock Down Publications

Email Us: We want to hear from you!

Prologue

It was a blazing afternoon in Quincy, Florida, as Zion shot across Pat Thomas Parkway en route home. This was one of them days where walking anywhere was out of the question, but he had a choice to either ride the bus home or walk. He decided to walk instead, because he didn't want to deal with De'Kari and his aggravating crew.

Not that Zion was a coward or anything, he just avoided problems he didn't want. All Zion cared for was playing football and going pro someday. Fortunately for him, he was the star running back for his high school football team. Standing at five-foot-ten, weighing a solid 190lbs., Zion was by far the third fastest prospect in his division. He was the county's golden child, the only senior who led their home team to the championship in ten years.

Zion Griffen was a beast on the field. He was a problem. Literally. You step in front of him, and you're bound to get run over. Big or small, Zion was gonna bring the pain on the field to whoever.

Meanwhile, the fierce June heat was bringing the pain of its own, and now Zion wished that he had rode the bus home instead. Suddenly, a horn honked behind him as a shiny red '24 Ford Mustang Dark Horse swerved alongside the road in front of him. Zion looked up in the direction of the car and paused for a brief second along the sidewalk.

"What's up, lil Zy! Hop in," said Quan, beckoning for Zion to slide in the passenger side so that he could get out the heat.

“I’m good, Q,” he said. “I’ma walk.”

“So you’re gonna walk all the way to Lake Skillet?”

Zion shrugged.

Quan continued. “C’mon, lil’ Zy. I’ma take you straight home. You family, my nigga. Plus, it’s too muthafuckin’ hot to be walkin’ anywhere. Get in the car and let’s slide, homeboy!”

Nine years ago Zion had lost his big brother Douvie to the streets. He was three years older than Zion. Shot and killed while standing on a street corner trying to hang out with the hustlaz. The victim of a drive-by shooting that left four people dead on that street corner. Since then, Zion’s mother had constantly warned him about interacting with the likes of street niggaz. His brother Douvie paid a price for his actions, and Zion refused to become another pain in his mother’s heart.

Now here it was—Quan, a well-known drug lord and a close friend of the family, one whose name was tied to murders and street influence, was offering him a ride home.

“Time is of the essence, lil’ Zy. Real shit,” Quan spoke up again. “It’s hot out here!”

After another moment of indecision, Zion tossed caution to the side and hurried over to get in the car. Quan reached over to deposit the brown leather backpack from the front seat into the back.

“Damn, nigga.” Quan smirked over at Zion as he slid onto the passenger seat beside him. “You act like we ain’t come up off the same turf or something.”

“We good,” Zion assured him.

“I know we good, my nigga. Now let’s get you home where you belong.”

But little did they know, neither one of them was gonna reach that destination anytime soon.

Chapter 1

Rashia was in the process of demolishing her chicken sandwich from McDonald's when the cellphone on top of the table in front of her rang. Licking her fingers clean, Rashia reached for her phone to answer it.

"Hello?" she replied.

"Hello. May I speak with Rashia Dawkins, please? This is an emergency," said the caller.

"This is Rashia. Who is this? And what's the emergency?" demanded Rashia, glancing down in her lap to make sure she hadn't dropped any food there.

She was wearing Prada and knew she had to be careful.

"I'm calling in regards to your grandmother, Hazel. She had been admitted here to the Quincy Hospital after taking a fall—"

Those was the last words Rashia heard before she bolted from the table straight for the exit of the restaurant. A minute later, Rashia was pulling out into traffic in her silver-colored Hyundai and racing toward the Quincy Hospital.

To hear that her grandmother was in trouble was all Rashia needed to hear to get herself in gear. This was the woman that raised her up in this cold world when her own mother failed to. Hazel Smith was her rock, her fortress, and for her, Rashia would trade her own life.

"I'm coming, mama," she whispered.

Then her heart became conflicted when a red light up ahead compromised her mission. She cussed and banged a fist against the steering wheel in total frustration. She then eased the car up behind a black SUV parked at the stop light.

Right at that moment the phone in her lap vibrated with an incoming text message. Rashia retrieved the phone and was about to read the text when the unexpected happen. There was movement out the corner of her eye, and Rashia glanced left to see what it was. Suddenly, the driver window exploded, and a pair of hands reached inside and took ahold of Rashia. Then she was snatched through the window and thrown to the ground.

"Shut the fuck up bitch!" sneered the assailant before the one standing next to him drew back and punched her in the face.

Then together, both goons dragged her toward the waiting car two links back and tossed her into the trunk. In broad daylight. Right in the middle of traffic at a red light.

Within the darkness of the trunk, Rashia screamed and banged out her fear and frustration against the confines of her prison. Then the car began moving and jerking her around in the trunk as it sped away from the scene in reckless haste.

"Please, God," Rashia prayed as thoughts of herself dying filled her consciousness.

Why she was being kidnapped she had no clue—only that whatever it was about, she hoped to not suffer. Then she thought about her grandmother.

"Oh no . . ." she grieved. "Mama!"

***

From the passenger side next to his homeboy, Zion looked over to see Quan lift up his red Solo cup to sip more of the brown liquor inside.

"So," Quan replied humbly, as Boston Richey poured from the sound system at a modest volume, "are we going to college or what?" he asked.

"*We*?" Zion had to catch himself. "Yeah. I applied for a few of them already. It's a waiting game for right now, though."

"Where did you apply to?"

"FSU. Bethune-Cookman. And Georgia State."

Quan nodded quietly. "They got some good programs, lil Zy. And to tell you the truth, I think somebody gon' pick you up before any of them calls you. With your type of stats, you supposed to have scouts beatin' down your front door right now," he said before lifting up his cup again.

"Whatchu know about my stats, Q?"

It didn't come as a surprise that Quan was a follower of his — Zion had many of them. He pretty much had his whole county and its surrounding areas rooting for him at every turn.

"Almost two thousand rushing yards, seventeen TDs, four assisted TDs. Nigga, I know your game. And I'm proud of you, Zy. Real shit," said Quan, with an outstretched hand towards Zion.

Zion looked down at his bejeweled fist and bumped it with his own.

"Damn, how I wish Spud could see you right now, dawg."

At the mention of his older cousin, who was now serving twenty years in prison for violent crimes, Zion dropped his head momentarily. Then he began to gaze out his side window in deep thought.

Two years ago, Spud was apprehended while out on the town with his girlfriend. He and Quan were homeboys. They grew up together running the streets and earning their keep. Spud was also one of Zion's biggest fans, next to his mother and his closest crony, Oscar. Zion and Oscar were more like brothaz from another mother, and he was the total opposite of Zion, which is why Quan probably liked him so much. Oscar was a fool. He was loyal.

"I promised bruh that I was gonna look out for you whenever I can," Quan stated.

"And you have, Q. You come to my games; you follow my career. That means more to me than anythang, big bro," said Zion.

When Quan opened his mouth to speak, he was interrupted by the blurp of a police siren behind them.

"Shit," he replied.

The police cruiser behind him hit its emergency lights but kept the siren quiet. It was a sure indication that he wanted Quan to pull over.

"What?" said Zion.

"The fuckin' police behind us," he said.

"Why?" Zion questioned, as a small bubble of panic grew inside of him.

Instead of answering his question, Quan reached beneath his seat where his Beretta 9mm was hidden. When Zion saw the gun, he instantly began to worry. All of a sudden, mental flashes of him and Quan being led away in cuffs invaded his thought process.

"Look, lil' Zy. I must pull this car over," said Quan. "But not with what I got inside. This is where I'ma need your help, my nigga."

"What you want me to do?" he asked.

"Grab that brown bookbag in the back behind you," said Quan.

Turning in his seat to look behind him, Zion spotted the brown leather backpack and grabbed it. It was a hefty bag by the heaviness of it. Now with the bag resting on his lap, Zion looked over to Quan for further instructions. Another blurp from the police car behind them alerted Quan that he needed to hurry. Any second now things could get crucial — and it was. Literally.

"Here." Quan then handed over the gun and then his cellphone to Zion, who in turn regarded him with obvious discontent.

"What I'm supposed to do with all this?" Zion asked him curiously.

"Run," Quan told him.

"Run?"

"Yeah. Run like you never ran before. Because what's in that bag you got cannot go into the wrong hands. I need you to protect that bag wit' your life, Zy. Please. Because another life is depending on it."

Peering into the rearview mirror at the police car behind them, Zion unconsciously placed his hand on the door handle.

"Wait until I say go," said Quan.

But Zion didn't have the patience for that, because just as sure as the car slowed down enough for retreat, Zion bolted from the seat like a human rocket. Once his feet touched ground, he was gone.

"Secure the bag, my nigga," muttered Quan, as he pulled the car over along the side of the road in the subdivision community.

When he looked back over, there was no sight of Zion anywhere. Quan smirked.

"Now what the fuck do you want wit' me, cracker?" He downed the rest of his Hennessy and waited to see what the universe brought him.

Chapter 2

Rashia was beside herself with both fear and madness when the car finally came to a halt some fifteen minutes later.

From her keen observation from within the trunk of the car, Rashia was rewarded a clue as to where she had been taken. A second ago, the car had stopped for a moment. Then came the unmistakable whine of what she guessed was a garage door lifting up on its rotors. Then came movement again, as the car lurched forward a few yards and stopped again.

Rashia believed she'd been taken to a warehouse of some sort. Wherever she was, she desperately wanted to be out of the trunk of the car.

No sooner than the thought crossed her mind did the doors to the car open and close shut almost in unison. Then, seconds later, there were voices outside the trunk of the car before it suddenly opened.

"Get the fuck out," said the big broad-shouldered goon whom Rashia remembered snatching her from the window of her car earlier.

Rashia looked up at the nigga in silent disdain, then shot a cautious glance over at his accomplice. He was shorter but stocky, not as gruff-looking as his partner.

"Don't make me tell you again, bitch," said the big guy, obviously the more aggressive one of the two. "Now!" he hissed.

Rising up to manage herself out of the trunk, Rashia guessed she wasn't moving fast enough. So big boy backhanded her across the face so hard it knocked her back down into the trunk. That's when he reached in with both hands and dragged her out.

"Get off me!" Rashia fought against him, kicking and screaming out her aggression.

What her abductors probably didn't know was that Rashia was far from just a pretty face. She grew up hard. She was a tough cookie to crack. Rashia was a fighter, never one to be bullied around or taken advantage of. So getting punched in the face wasn't anything new to her. She could take a lick or two, but not without striking out to get her lick back.

"Sit your ass down." Big boy slammed her onto the floor hard.

Then he reached up to his face, where Rashia had clawed his flesh.

"You bitch!" he growled menacingly at her.

Seeing the murderous scowl on his face, Rashia distanced herself by crawling backward as he moved toward her.

"Stay away from me," she told him.

After a few more feet in retreat, Rashia felt her body collide with something solid behind her. The impact sent a big, heavy tool wrench tumbling down onto her. First it struck her shoulder, then landed in her lap, where it remained.

Quickly, Rashia reached for the steel wrench and took possession of it.

That's when big boy pulled out his .45 caliber and snarled in her direction.

"Now whatchu gon' do with that, bitch?" he said, brandishing the gun before her.

Although he had a gun in his hand and her weapon was just a wrench, Rashia knew he wasn't gonna shoot her. She was smart enough to know that if they wanted her dead, she would have died back at the traffic scene.

So instead of cowering, Rashia picked herself up and faced off with her enemy. That's when she realized there were more than just two goons involved. There were two more present, one of them Rashia recognized by face but not by name.

“I should kill your stupid ass right now,” said the big goon as he stood before her like a huge boulder.

Right then, the garage door whined again as it slowly rose to allow another vehicle to enter. It was then that Rashia noticed she had been brought to a mechanic shop. All types of car parts and whatnots filled the large garage. Not one Rashia had ever been to, but one all the same.

The vehicle that rolled into the shop was a pearl-white ’23 Maserati MC20. At the sight of the car, Rashia automatically knew who it belonged to, because there was only one person in the whole area who owned such a ride.

Donte Jones.

Sure enough, that’s exactly who it was when he stepped from the car.

A lump formed in Rashia’s throat when the stone-cold killer she knew Donte as swiveled his gaze in her direction.

“What the hell is this, Moon?” said Donte, his attention on the big guy.

He approached the group alongside his right-hand man, Killah, whose reputation was just as profound as his.

“We got the bitch you wanted,” Moon said.

“Oh, really?” Donte sneered darkly. “Does she look white to you, nigga? And does she have short dark hair to you, fool?”

When Moon looked over at Rashia, his eyes clouded with pure hate.

“I told that nigga that’s the wrong bitch,” said Tank, the second goon whom Rashia had the displeasure of meeting as well.

“Isn’t that so?” Donte replied.

Tank shrugged.

That was Rashia’s cue to speak up.

"Good," she said. "It appears I'm not the one you're lookin' for. So can I please leave now? I swear I won't say a thang. My word. I just wanna go home," she pleaded.

Donte swiftly drew his sidearm, a chrome automatic pistol, and aimed it directly at Moon's face.

"You played, nigga."

Rashia gasped.

Blocka!

One shot was all it took to drop Moon where he stood. Before his body hit the floor, Donte was already turning his attention back to Rashia's piercing brown eyes.

"Now give me one good reason why I should let you leave here alive," said Donte, and Rashia would've sworn she saw the devil in that nigga's eyes.

***

Yvonnie was shifting into a better position on the plush sofa to sleep in when the phone sounded off.

"Who is this?" she answered groggily when she didn't recognize the number.

"This Cody from Friendship," said the caller on the other end.

"Okay?" Yvonnie yawned.

"I don't know what's going on, but them people just took Quan in just now," he said.

Yvonnie was now sitting upright on the sofa after hearing those words. Then she demanded that Cody elaborate further on what he knew.

Whoever this Cody from Friendship was, he was on his way home riding on a school bus when he spotted Quan's car. He witnessed a police car with its lights on demanding that Quan pull over. Then someone bolted from the car with a brown bag in his possession.

That's what really brought Yvonnie to her feet at once — the mention of the brown bag. The very same brown bag that she herself filled with the contents from Quan's safe. A total of three hundred and fifty thousand dollars meant to go toward the financing of his mother's heart transplant.

Twenty minutes ago, that's where Quan left her to go — to meet up with the people responsible for saving his mother's life. Now here it was, Yvonnie being told someone other than the people the money was meant for had it in their possession.

"Did you get a good look at the person who got away wit' that bag?" she asked.

From the other end of the phone, Yvonnie heard Cody conversing with somebody else in regard to the question she asked.

"Cody!"

"Um . . . they say it was Zion," he said.

"Who the fuck is they!" she shouted into the phone. "Never mind. Zion. I got it."

"It looked like a setup to me," added Cody.

A setup.

Quan was in trouble. Zion. The money bag. All of that equaled blood and murder if she had anything to do with it.

It didn't take her long to put some clothes on and equip herself with some firepower. Then she was out the door, into her Lexus Jeep, headed for the location where she was told Quan was last seen.

Then she called up the goon squad.

Shit was about to get hectic. Dangerous even.

And Yvonnie had no understanding when it came down to her man. She loved his mother, true enough, but Quan was her world.

That weakness would get you killed.

Chapter 3

For four minutes, Zion had run as hard as he could, distancing himself from whatever fate belied Quan. He went from running like he had the Grim Reaper on his tail, to jumping fences and taking shortcuts through paths and trails to reach his destination.

That destination was home on Hamilton Street in the hood of Lake Skillet — five houses down from where Quan grew up.

By the time Zion made it home and inside the house, he was dead tired. The blazing heat was beating down on his body, along with all the extra activity he had to go through to get there.

Zion dropped down onto the couch and tried to catch his breath. Then a thought came to mind, and he was back on his feet, turning up the air system in the house. From there, he went into the kitchen, where he downed two cups of cold water. Then he topped it off with a cup of orange juice.

"Damn," he sighed with pleasure.

Standing there in the kitchen, staring into space, Zion wondered how Quan was faring. Then he thought back on Quan's last words before he found himself back in the living room, staring down at the leather backpack and the gun, which was now resting next to it.

Zion couldn't believe he had been running around town clutching a semiautomatic weapon like he was some gangster. He could just imagine what people were saying when they witnessed this.

Just that thought alone worried him — whether it would affect his football career or not.

"What's in the bag?"

Zion reached to unzip the backpack to see what was inside.

When the bag was opened and he peered inside, Zion gasped at all the money he saw within it. He took up one of the money stacks bound with rubber bands and inspected it up close. He'd never seen this much money at one time. Having it in his possession now scared him.

No wonder Quan wanted him to protect it with his life. It was probably his earnings from street hustling all these years.

Minutes later, while in his bedroom, Zion took the liberty to transfer the money from one bag to another. He had found his old JanSport backpack in the back of his closet and decided to use that one instead.

That's when he heard it — a car pulling up outside, by the squeaking of its brakes being administered. Zion hurried up front to see who it was, because his mother didn't get off work until five, so he knew it wasn't her.

"Oh shit!" Zion backed away from the window when he saw the three armed goons bounding from the car parked out front at the curb.

They were heading straight for the front door.

Zion spun and ran for his bedroom, where he snatched up the bag and gun and dashed for the window to escape.

When the front door was kicked in, Zion was halfway out the window.

One of the gunmen entered the bedroom just as Zion dropped down onto the earth. The gunman reached out and aimed, sending four shots in Zion's direction. One of those bullets zoomed just past his right ear before he bent the corner around the back of the house.

Once again, Zion was running for his life.

But that's what he was good at doing.

Running. Putting distance between him and his opponents.
It was the story of his life.
To run.

***

The stakes were high, and Rashia knew that in order for her to survive this situation she would have to be damn convincing. Fear was not an option. She was in the presence of killaz, and there was no room for fear.

"I'm waitin'," said Donte.

He stood there in his Italian threads and loafers, humble but also menacing in a way.

"You say one good reason, right?" she asked, and Donte nodded.

At that point, the rest of Donte's men began to fan out as though they expected the very same action she was about to take. That's when Rashia focused her attention on the one named Tank. The same nigga who punched her in the face back at the traffic scene.

"So what's it gonna be?" said Killah, obviously impatient and wanting to be shown what type of bitch he was in the presence of.

"Okay," muttered Rashia readily.

Then with that same tool wrench she was clutching, she rushed Tank hard with it. He flinched instinctively when Rashia lifted the weapon.

"You put your fuckin' hands on me!" she swung the wrench, and it connected with the side of his face.

Killah frowned and moved forward to intervene, but Donte stiff-armed him and told Killa to fall back and let her do her thing.

By this time, Rashia had followed up with her first blow and dropped Tank with the second one. When he hit the floor, Rashia fell on top of him and began bashing his face with the weapon.

"Dee?" said Spider, one of the other goons who stood amongst them. "She gon' kill'em!"

Donte didn't even acknowledge him.

In her rage, Rashia had blacked out for a minute before she realized what she was doing. Then she ceased her actions.

Rashia stared down at Tank and saw only a bloody mess. There was blood all over her clothes and face.

"You done now?" Donte finally spoke up, seeing that Tank wasn't actually dead, but he damn sure looked like he was.

Lifting her gaze up at Donte, she climbed up off Tank to go stand before him. Donte did not shy away from the bloody mess Rashia had become during the midst of her rage. Something in her changed during those moment and it shone in her brown eyes.

"Can I go now, Donte?" she asked.

"Not just yet," he said.

At hearing those words Rashia clenched the bloody wrench in her grasp.

"Not yet?"

"You'll be taking a major risk leaving somebody like Tank alive," said Donte. "Especially after what you did to him. Yeah, you fucked him up real good, but wounds heal in due time—"

"Shut up, Donte!" snapped Rashia before taking his gun away from him and turning back towards Tank. He was indeed fucked up.

Both Killah and Donte looked at each other.

Rashia said, "Me or you, nigga," then she aimed the gun at Tank's head and pulled the trigger, killing him where he lay. "I chose me." Rashia looked away from the gory scene she had just created.

Then without so much a glance in Donte's direction, she moved for the exit of the garage and let herself out. Once she was back outside and free of the threat to vomit by looking at Tank. Rashia took big gulps of breath of fresh air.

For a long moment, she just stood there reflecting on what had just taken place. She wanted so bad to go back in there and shoot every last one of them, but instead she looked forward and took off running away from there. Thoughts of her grandmother's well-being resurfaced, and that was the energy she took from. Rashia ran hard as she could run. To reach her grandmother was her only focus.

After a while, Rashia came to the realization that she was still in possession of Donte's gun and the bloody wrench. So she ducked off into a nearby alleyway between an old laundromat building and a tire shop. There, Rashia disposed of the wrench down inside the gutter drain behind the laundromat. She was about to do the same with the gun until a sense of cautiousness washed over her.

Keep the gun for safety purposes, Rashia told herself, and then tucked it in her waistline behind her to conceal it.

"I gotta get rid of this shirt," she said.

Rashia pulled off her blood-stained blouse and shook her head wearily.

"Fuckin' Prada," she muttered and entered the laundromat, only to find nobody inside—but there were clothes in the process of being washed.

With a quick scan of the area outside the building, Rashia did not see who was responsible of washing the clothes. Whoever it was, probably across the street at the corner store. That was all the indication she needed to toss her bloody shirt into the washer with the other clothes. Then she plundered through the basket on the laundry counter and came up with a burgundy T-shirt.

"It'll do for now," she said.

Moments after putting the T-shirt on, in walked the last person Rashia expected to see.

"Rah Rah?" said Tranay Chandler, an old friend of hers she'd known since high school.

"Gurl, am I happy to see you right now."

"What're you doing wit' my shirt on?" Tranay replied.

Rashia shrugged. "It's complicated.

"It's dirty," she said. "It hasn't been washed yet."

Little did Tranay know, Rashia didn't have time to socialize; she was on a mission. So she told Tranay what she needed most.

"Of course, I'll take you to the hospital," she said.

"Thank you," sighed Rashia.

But for some reason, she felt like it was already too late.

Chapter 4

After hearing the gunshots ring out behind him, Zion turned the jets on. He bent the corner around the back of the house and shot straight across the neighbor's backyard.

That was ten minutes ago.

Now Zion found himself hiding behind the old gray metal shed behind Mr. Buster's house. Everybody in the neighborhood knew if there's one person you don't want to cross in the hood, it was Mr. Buster. The old man was a war hero, shell-shocked even, and didn't take too kindly to people trampling over his property.

This was one of those desperate moments for Zion. He was more willing to welcome the old man's wrath than face the three goons who were after him with guns.

Zion's chest pounded like it was trying to break out of him. His breath came in short, shaky bursts, and his palms were slick with sweat as he crouched lower behind the shed. Every sound — a car door slamming, a dog barking down the block — made him flinch. He kept replaying the gunshots in his head, the sharp pops echoing like they were still happening. He'd never been that close to death before. Never in his life had anyone shot at him. It was so surreal. It was mind-blowing just knowing you could be dead. Speaking of which, Zion removed the backpack from his back to examine it. During his flee from the shooter, he had felt something punch him in the back. If he wasn't careful he would have lost his footing from the impact.

"Goddamn." Zion was taken aback by the bullet hole he spotted in front of the backpack.

He rubbed a finger across the hole and knew if it wasn't for the money inside, he would be severely injured or dead.

Opening the backpack to get inside, Zion blindly sifted through the multiple bundles of cash until he located the one he was searching for. When he had it in front of him with the bullet still embedded into the money, Zion wanted to kiss it gratefully.

Right then, he heard the back door to Mr. Buster's house open, and then came the unmistakable bark of Shocker. Shocker was Mr. Buster's full-blooded pit bull terrier, and he didn't play no games.

"Gimme a fuckin' break, please!" Zion risked a look around the corner of the shed.

Shocker was heading his way and coming fast. It had to be Shocker, thought Zion, as he took off running into the woods behind the shed.

Shocker had to have alerted the old man that an intruder was on their grounds somehow.

"Don't let 'em get away, boy!" Zion heard Mr. Buster yell out after his beast of a dog.

As for Shocker, the old man fed him so much that his massiveness took away from his speed. By the time Shocker cleared the threshold of the woods, Zion was already ten yards ahead. Not to brag, but he was faster than Shocker. That was the old man's mistake.

It didn't take long before Zion finally came upon a gate behind another residence and scaled it with ease. From there, he made his way towards the front and was letting himself out its front entrance before he was stopped.

"Where are you going, Zion?"

Turning a glance over his shoulder at the voice—and to his surprise—it was his cousin Kelli standing in the doorway of the house. Another body appeared in the doorway behind her, and he felt his heart skip a beat. It was Candice Brown.

The girl of his dreams. His childhood crush. Candice also had a boyfriend, and his name was Jamir. Jamir was the best friend of Zion's archenemy: De'Kari.

This wasn't either one of the girls' home; it actually belonged to MiMi Rogers.

"C'mere, cuz." Kelli beckoned him over with a wave, and Zion hesitated.

Then, just up the street, passed two cars headed from Hamilton Street towards MLK. The second car was the very same one Zion saw outside his house before all hell broke loose. Now, standing out there in front of MiMi's house left him exposed. His best bet was to find a safe shelter—even if it meant being in the company of Candice.

As he turned for the house, Zion looked up to see Candice smirking at him.

Then Shocker showed up again. He was coming along the other side of the fence toward the entrance of the gate. Zion was halfway across the front yard when the dog suddenly charged through the gate at him.

"Fuck!" Zion ran for the front door of the house as both girls goaded him on.

He damn near had to dive through the door to get inside. Kelli shut the door as fast as she could. Then, when she turned to face her cousin, Zion was stretched out on the floor of the foyer at Candice's feet. Outside the front door, Shocker was barking up a storm. Zion picked himself up off the floor, and together they moved into the living room.

"What do you got going on, Zy?" asked Kelli, her and Candice sharing the same sofa.

With his head in his hands, Zion lifted his head up and said, "I'm in trouble, cuz."

"How?"

"Because of what you did to Quan?" Candice interjected, and Kelli elbowed her in the side.

"I ain't do nothing to Quan," he said.

"That's not what the streets are saying," Kelli replied, pulling out her cellphone.

Now Zion felt like snapping.

"I don't know what's going on!" he said.

"Then what's in the bag?" Candice asked.

Zion looked at the bag he now had resting at his feet.

"Nothing."

Should he tell them the truth?

"*Protect that bag with your life, Zy.*"

Those were Quan's exact words. So no, he wouldn't tell them, because just as soon as he did, all types of shit was bound to go wrong. He couldn't risk that.

No one is to be trusted.

***

When Yvonnie located Quan's car near the Sub-Division area, it was parked along the side of the road and empty. The doors were locked, so she couldn't get in.

"Damn, bae," she muttered to herself as she shielded her hands around her eyes to peer into the windows of the car.

There was no bag present inside.

Right at that moment, a Triple-A vehicle pulled up on the scene. Yvonnie looked up at the truck as the driver angled its rear before the front of the Mustang. Sneering darkly, Yvonnie made her way over to the big truck.

"Leave it be," she told the heavy-looking white guy getting out the truck.

"Excuse me?" he said.

Drawing her weapon and cocking it back to chamber a round, Yvonnie said, "Unless you want a bullet in your fuckin' head, I suggest you get back in that truck and go."

"But—" he stammered.

"No buts." Yvonnie put the gun to his wide forehead. "Leave," she said.

The driver hopped back up behind the wheel of his truck and roared away.

Yvonnie's cellphone rang, and she answered it briskly.

"What?"

"We missed him," the caller said.

Yvonnie responded, "The fuck you mean you missed him, Trill!" she fumed. "Missed him how?" Her tone was cold as ice.

Trill explained to her how he, Rocko, and Prep pulled up on the scene and kicked the door in. Somehow, Zion got wind of the move and was dropping out the bedroom window when Prep sent shots after him.

"Then me and Rocko hit the back door after him, but by that time he was already gone," Prep said.

"The little nigga run like a cheetah!" said Trill.

"They say he's a star athlete."

"He is," Trill replied.

"Fuck that. Find him, Trill," she said. "Get everybody on it. It's crucial that we recover that bag he has before it's too late."

"What's wit' that fuckin' bag anyway, sis?"

"Never mind that, Trill."

"Just get it," he said.

She nodded.

"Exactly."

Then Yvonnie disconnected them as a new thought came to mind. Having wasted more than enough time already, Yvonnie materialized with the spare key to Quan's car attached to her own key ring. She got in and shut the door, then she put a call in through to Sheena.

Sheena was a certified smacker—one of the few bitches that Yvonnie trusted. She always said when Yvonnie needed her, she was just a phone call away.

"What's the issue?" Sheena picked up the phone on the second ring.

"What makes you think there's an issue?"

"That's the only time you call me," said Sheena with a hint of sass.

"Well," Yvonnie replied with a sigh, "I need you right now, Sheena."

"I know."

"His name is Zion Griffen."

"I know."

Yvonnie paused.

"You know?"

"Yeah. And I'm not touchin' him, Yvonnie."

"Why?" she asked.

"Because," Sheena said, "Zion is my little cousin. And I'm going all out 'bout him. So please be warned," she expressed.

Then the line disconnected. Sheena was gone.

There was nothing else to talk about.

Chapter 5

By the time Rashia made it to the hospital, her nerves were shot. She had no understanding for nothing. All she wanted was her grandmother, and by all means she better be alive. Upon entering the hospital, Rashia marched right up to the information desk. Luckily for her, it was somebody she already knew manning the desk. She demanded to know where her grandmother was.

"What's her name?" asked T. Haines, which was the name printed on her nameplate.

"Hazel Matthews," she said.

"Just a sec."

"Never mind all that mess," said another voice just beyond Rashia's left shoulder. "I'll take you to Hazel myself," he said with earnest.

When Rashia turned at the familiar voice, she was not even surprised to see Hank Dennis standing before her. This was Hazel's longtime friend and former crush from back in the day when she was young and thriving. Hank also lived just up the road from Rashia's beloved grandmother.

"Take me to her," she replied.

"My pleasure," Hank beckoned her to follow him.

En route to the room where Hazel was being kept, Rashia inquired about her grandmother's condition. About a year ago, Hazel had a minor heart attack, and it just about killed Rashia too. Now to hear that her grandmother has had another one was really pulling on Rashia's heartstrings.

"She also fractured her hip when she fell from the front porch," he said.

He had been on his own front porch loading up his old tackle box when he looked up and noticed Hazel on the ground.

"She broke her hip?" Rashia paused.

"Fractured."

"Same damn thang." Rashia frowned. "She can't walk on her own now. She would have to get around in a wheelchair now," she said with a sigh.

"Which brings me to my next concern."

Rashia looked over at him.

"I think it's time that you commit her to the senior citizen assisted living program they got over there in Triple Oaks."

"The old folks home?"

Hank shrugged.

"She'll get the help she needs there, Rashia. A full ride of assistance."

Before she cussed him out for suggesting such a thing, Rashia walked off from him. She made it only a couple of yards before she realized she didn't exactly know what room her grandmother was in. Without a word, Hank pressed forward and gestured up the hall for her to follow.

A minute later they stopped outside the room door where Hazel was occupying. Rashia reached for the door to go inside, but a hand gripped ahold of her arm to stop her.

"What?" Rashia snapped at him.

"I don't know what your trouble was before you got here, but you can't take it in there wit' you, Rashia."

"What're you talkin' about, Hank?"

"You got blood in your eyes," he said. "And I can smell the blood on you."

His words made Rashia look down at herself, but she couldn't see any blood. That's when she entered the room and was about to make a quick entrance into the adjoining bathroom until she glanced left and spotted her grandmother.

"Mama," she whispered.

Hank watched as Rashia briskly approached her grandmother's bed and came to rest at her bedside. Rashia stared down upon her sleeping face, which was protruded with an oxygen tube, and felt her whole world shatter to pieces.

"Oh, mama," she cried softly, reaching forward to stroke her short, curly hair.

"She's stronger than she looks," he said.

But that's not what Rashia was thinking; she knew the woman lying before her was one tough cookie. Rashia was thinking about Tank at that moment, the nigga whose life she had taken. Somehow, she felt she had to take a life in order for her grandmother to live, and she would do it again. If it meant killing more just for her grandmother to stay alive, then she would most definitely do so. It was a fucked-up way of thinking. Rashia was serious. She loved that old woman just that much to play God with the rest of the world.

***

The car in which Oscar pulled up in was a shiny black Infiniti Q30 that he legitimately paid for with the money he'd accumulated from his last two licks. He parked the car outside Zion's house with the intentions of taking him out to Dairy Queen to meet up with his girl Joya and her cousin Bre. This was Zion's best friend since elementary, the boy who lived around the corner whose mother was a well-known trick in town. It was Oscar whom Zion actually called his brother. Even his mother looked at him as her son, despite the fact that he was living a worrisome lifestyle.

Oscar was different. He had come from a broken home where all he knew was pain and being a dog. If it wasn't for Zion and his loved ones, Oscar would have been lost a long time ago. It was Oscar who came home later that night with blood all over his clothes after Douvie got killed. He had gone after the person whom he thought was responsible, but after not finding him, Oscar took it to his brother Tyleek, whom he knew from school. That night, Tyleek was beaten severely with a baseball bat in the neighborhood park. That's what won Tabitha Williams over to Oscar after what he did in honor of her son. He was just ten years old at the time, a year older than Zion, and his loyalty was without question.

Oscar got out his new car on Hamilton Street and readjusted the black and gray Raiders fitted cap over his eyes to block the sun. Then he made his way towards the front door of the house. It was then that he noticed the front door opened, but to his trained eye, it wasn't left open by mistake. It looked forced, and that's all the indication Oscar needed to snap into beast mode.

Just as he was reaching to retrieve the gun from his waistline, the front door to the neighbor's house next door opened and Matilda Shaw stepped outside.

"He's not in there, Oscar," said Matilda.

"What happened?" he asked.

Oscar figured if she knew Zion wasn't home, then she knew more about why the front door was hanging off the hinges. Matilda descended the porch steps and beckoned Oscar over to where she came to rest on the other side of the gate separating the two homes. Matilda was much older, probably mid-twenties, but cool as hell. She had a thing for young niggaz, and Oscar had already smashed her fine ass twice. The young nigga was a beast. He had his fat boy swag thing going on, and the women found that alluring in a sense, and Oscar took advantage of every single opportunity.

"What'z up wit' my brotha, Matilda?" said Oscar once he stepped over the gate.

"I don't really know," she said. "But I know it was Prep and Trill who was involved."

Matilda then went to explain that she was in her bedroom changing clothes when she heard the first gunshot blast. That's what brought her to her bedroom window to look outside, and that's when she saw Prep standing inside of Zion's bedroom window, blazing shots after him. That shit had Oscar boiling inside.

"I think one of them bullets hit him too."

"What!" Oscar panicked.

Then he broke away from her to go investigate the scene. He walked alongside Zion's house toward his bedroom window, and that's when he saw the shattered bedroom window from which the bullet hole still was pronounced. Then he glanced in the direction that Zion had ran, staring down at the ground, searching for blood.

The back door was also opened, and Oscar assumed it was because Zion's adversaries had begun to take chase after him.

"Couldn't catch him if you tried," muttered Oscar before entering the house through the back door.

The house was quiet as a mouse. Oscar drew his gun and went through every room in search of whatever it was he needed to see. The house wasn't trashed or ransacked. They had come for one thing, and that was his brother.

"But why Zion?" wondered Oscar.

Minutes afterwards, Oscar exited through the front door after forcing it back shut. Also standing outside the house now was Jabari, aka Jabo, who lived up the street from there.

"You ain't heard the latest news, O?" said Jabo, a young hoodlum whom Oscar knew well but tries too hard to be accepted.

"What's the news?" he asked.

"That your brotha Zee set Quan up and got him arrested."

Oscar shook his head and stepped forward to place his gun against the lips of Jabo's mouth.

"Saying some dumb shit like that would get you killed, Jabo. My brotha ain't set nobody up! And whoever got a problem wit' that shit, tell them to come see me," he sneered darkly.

Right at that moment, a Mazda CX-90 pulled up on the scene and its driver-side window rolled down. A cloud of smoke poured out from within.

"Yo, Oscar," said Sheena, calling out from behind the wheel.

He glanced over and frowned, then turned his gaze back on Jabo.

"Get the fuck from round here, Jabo, before I let loose on your ass."

And Jabo got missing, hurrying away from Oscar and the murderous glaze in his dark eyes. Then Oscar made his way over to the car and got in.

"You won't believe the bullshit I just heard," said Oscar, accepting the nice blunt of Loud that Sheena was smoking on.

"I already heard about it," Sheena told him.

"Whatchu heard?" he asked.

Because from the looks of things, Oscar believed a war had been initiated, and he was about to go berserk. Zion was in trouble. Niggaz was really out there lurking on him, and Oscar only saw blood when it came to that point. There would be no remorse given because they shouldn't have fucked with him in the first place.

Chapter 6

MiMi was sitting on the edge of her bed, her face bent forward towards the line of Molly powder she had made for herself onto the little vanity hand mirror in front of her. Zion shook his head sadly as he stood outside her bedroom looking in. Then he proceeded on into the bathroom across the hall from her room. He had known his cousin Kelli was a Molly head but not MiMi. MiMi was the last person Zion expected to indulge in drugs, and surely not Candice. He knew without a shadow of a doubt Candice didn't indulge herself but only looked out for her friends whenever they were in the midst of doing it.

In the bathroom, Zion relieved himself as he reflected on the tension he left back in the room up front. Both Kelli and Candice tried to get him to confess his sins to them when he had none to confess. Zion told them straight up to shut the fuck up about it and let him think it all over. No sooner than he began relieving himself did he hear the front door close shut at the voice of none other than Jamir Copeland, and from that voice, Zion heard his name being mentioned as Candice responded back in that stubborn way of hers.

Right at that moment, Zion knew some bullshit was about to go down. He finished peeing and was about to hit the back door to escape until he saw De'Kari standing at the mouth of the hallway. It wasn't so much as De'Kari's presence that moved him; it was the unmistakable sound of a palm striking flesh, and Candice cried out in result.

"Here that fool go right here," shouted De'Kari, pointing a finger in his direction.

Instead of backing out of the situation this time, Zion met it head-on. He marched right up the hallway towards his archenemy.

"De'Kari, get off her!" said Kelli. "She wasn't doing nothin' wit' him. Stop!"

"Shouldn't've had that punk in here anyway," De'Kari retorted as he continued to rough Candice up from the sounds of struggling transpiring.

Right when Zion was in striking reach, De'Kari gave that little evil smirk of his and struck out at him with a punch to the face. Zion weaved the blow and stiff-armed him hard in the chest, causing De'Kari to stumble off balance.

"Zee!" Kelli called out to her cousin with plea in her eyes for help.

There was another one of De'Kari's boys present; his name was Duke, and when he saw Zion charging forward, he moved clearly out of the way. Jamir had Candice pinned down on the sofa as she tried to remove herself from under his brute aggressiveness. Zion saw this and tackled Jamir so hard that he scooped him up off of the sofa and body slammed him into the floor. The vicious impact of their bodies colliding against the floor shook the whole house.

"Damn," was all Kelli could say.

"The fuck you standing there lookin' stupid for!" replied De'Kari, shoving Duke forward as he too shot forward to go after Zion.

Together they pounced right on top of him, punching Zion and kicking him.

"Oh hell naw!" Kelli removed her earrings and jumped in to help her cousin.

By the time MiMi made it up front, the living room was already turned into a battleground, and even Candice jumped in to help her friend as she and Kelli were putting a licking on Duke together. When MiMi saw this, she just knew her mother was going to kill her when she got home.

Then the unexpected happened.

As Zion was battling it out with De'Kari and Jamir, the backpack he had strapped to his back was somehow torn during the struggle. In the process, some of its contents spilled out the bag onto the floor.

When Zion realized this, he panicked and hurriedly reached for the Beretta .9mm. By this time, the battle had ceased when the money came pouring out the bag. Even Duke, with a busted nose and a gradually blackening eye, stepped forward to pick up one of the money stacks.

"Put it down, Duke," said Zion, raising the gun to aim it at him steadily.

Candice was looking stuck on stupid.

"So you robbed Quan for real?" said De'Kari, with astonishment written all on his face.

"Don't make me tell you again, Duke," warned Zion, as he stepped forward to snatch the money out of Duke's hand. "Everybody back up!" he said.

"Man," De'Kari said with the smack of his lips. "You ain't gonna shoot nobody wit' that gun."

Then he knelt down to retrieve one of the money stacks.

Blocka!

The blast from the gun startled them all, even Zion, who had sent a bullet into the floor nearest De'Kari where he was. The impact of the bullet striking the floor instantly sent De'Kari falling back on his ass.

Now the gun had everybody's attention, but it was the person who had the gun that really shocked them all. Never in a million years had they imagined Zion Griffen brandishing a loaded weapon.

"Don't kill us, Zee. I'm sorry, man," said Jamir, backing towards the front door.

"That's right," Zion said grimly. "Go. Run! Get the fuck outta this house right now!" He aimed the Beretta from one hoodlum to the other, demanding them to get from out of his eyesight.

De'Kari, Jamir, and Duke all but trampled over one another running out the front door. Seeing this rewarded Zion a small sense of pride, but the tension in the air was still thick.

"My mama is gonna fuck me up for sure now," said MiMi, more worried about being grounded than the actual situation that just transpired.

Zion began collecting all the money that had fallen from the bag and putting it back inside. Unafraid of what Zion was now capable of doing, Candice still moved forward to help him with the task to resecure the money into the bag.

"That bag is busted, cuz," noticed Kelli.

"Yeah," he answered warily. "I see that."

Zion was now holding the backpack with both hands to prevent any more money from spilling out.

"I hope you know where that shit is about to go now, Zion?" said Kelli. "What you just did . . . Jamir no doubt is about to go tell his big brotha. And we all know how stupid Loony is."

With that notion, Zion was sure to go through it now if Loony got involved. Loony was affiliated with the new chapter of Gangster Disciples that was running their small town now after Hooliganz Crime Gang had died off into nothing but a lasting memory of Quincy, Florida's most deadliest organization that ever existed. Loony was a serious problem that Zion wanted no dealings with. It was already a problem trying to survive the killaz who were already gunning for him. With Loony after him too, it was indeed a state of emergency, and Zion only had one great option.

Call Oscar.

"Here you go." MiMi had left and returned with her own backpack, offering it to Zion to use now that his was ruined.

Quickly, Zion deposited the money from one bag to the other. Then he remembered the stash of money he'd pocketed earlier back at his house. Reaching into his front pocket, Zion felt the embedded bullet still resting in the fold of bills. When he removed the money stash, he unbound it from the rubber band securing it. The bullet fell onto the floor once the money was unfolded of its hold.

Kelli picked it up.

"What's this, Zion?"

"A bullet," he said.

Zion then peeled away two one-hundred-dollar bills and handed them over to MiMi to compensate her troubles. Then he handed both his cousin and Candice a $100 each for their loyalty to him for what they did.

"Thank you," said Candice humbly.

As he was stuffing the money back into his pocket, once again the front door was kicked in. Instinct brought the Beretta up, and Zion shot the first person that stepped through the door. Then he dashed for the rear of the house before the body even hit the floor.

Behind him, more shots were heard on top of petrified screams coming from the girls left up front. Hearing those horrifying cries as death settled upon them made Zion believe that he was next to die along with them.

So he ran harder.

Out the rear patio door he went, literally crashing through the glass door in his desperate fleet to get away from his adversaries.

Once again, Zion raced for the back gate and leapt over that muthafucker like Pookie did in *New Jack City* running from twelve, and back into the woods he went. This time with the courage to pull the trigger if need be. If Shocker showed his face again, Zion was gonna blow it clean off for him. There was no more playing.

The pressure was on. People were dying now.

***

"Hold up! Shit! Look at this shit!" Oscar pointed up the street where he saw a brown box Chevy Caprice idling outside MiMi Rogers' house.

But it's what he saw happening outside the house that made Oscar suspect Zion was involved.

"Right on time," said Sheena, reaching for the Glock 19 resting in her lap.

Outside the house was Prep and Rocko, who were in the process of half-carrying a bloody Trill across the front lawn towards the car. He appeared to be shot somewhere in the stomach area, and there was blood all over them.

Oscar ordered her to stop the car, and he hopped out at once. Oscar didn't even hesitate blasting shots in their direction as he rushed towards them. For a fat boy, Oscar surely moved with impressive speed and stealth as he let loose on them in front of him. Meanwhile, Sheena was dumping hot slugs into the driver-side door of the Chevy Caprice. She had that fool trapped and was filling his body up with holes.

During this time, Oscar had shot and killed Trill and Rocko, as Prep took off running along the side of the house out of sight. He didn't have the guts to blaze it out in honor of those he had come on this mission with.

"Bitch ass nigga!" Oscar yelled after him as Prep disappeared around the corner of the house.

Then Oscar rushed for the front door of the house only to find a bloody mess inside, but surprisingly, Candice was the only one still breathing. Oscar knew it was Zion's secret sweet love and felt sorry for her. Candice had been shot twice in the neck and chest, and her will to fight to live was amazing.

"Zee . . ." she managed to release as her life force drained from her body from her two wounds.

Candice stared at Oscar with glossy eyes of raw fear and approaching death. Oscar left her there bleeding to death to go check the rest of the house. That's when he discovered the broken patio door and stepped through it to look outside.

Suddenly, a capture of movement at his right instantly made him bring his gun up, and he squeezed off multiple shots at Prep fleeing the scene once again. This time Prep shot back at him as he dashed for the back gate and over it into the thick of the woods beyond. Refusing to chase after him, Oscar hurried back around the house into the car with Sheena, and they peeled out from the murder scene.

"Did you get him?"

"No," Oscar shook his head as they came upon the end of Flager Street, and that's when he saw De'Kari, Jamir, and Duke all posted up on the front porch looking out at them.

"Hold on, Sheena," he said.

Then Oscar opened the car door, stepped out, and sent a series of hot slugs at the three hoodlums. One of them dropped, and the others dispersed.

"What was that about?" asked Sheena when they were back in traffic moments later.

"A warning to them niggaz not to fuck wit' my brotha again," said Oscar.

He confided in her that he knew Zion was weary of De'Kari and his crew, which Zion failed to express to Oscar because he knew how destructive he could get in regard to his well-being.

"So they bully him around then?"

"Not exactly," said Oscar. "Zee just don't wanna deal wit' them fools because of what they be doing to everybody else. But whether they know it or not, I like Zee to chump all three of them."

"Well," Sheena said. "You just did it for him."

"We need to find my brotha."

"Most definitely."

"Oh yeah. And Sheena?"

She heard the sound in his voice and glanced over at Oscar.

"What is it, Oscar?"

"Kelli," he said. "She was in that house too. They had killed her and both of her friends."

No words came from Sheena after that, only a lone tear sliding down her face, and that was the wrong thing to do to someone of her caliber.

Make her cry. It was like shooting yourself in the heart.

Chapter 7

For almost an hour now, Quan had been freezing his ass off in the interrogation room located downstairs of the old Quincy Police Station. His left hand was cuffed to the arm of the metal chair, which was bolted down to the floor. Across from him was a two-way mirror, in which he knew was a sitting room for officials to witness the goings-on in the interrogation room.

Quan could think of a number of reasons why he was now sitting in that cold room. He was a gangster, a reputed drug lord, and with that title came a lot of bloodshed and experience. As far as his street sense was concerned, Quan was smart enough not to leave a trail behind whatever he did in the streets, and it couldn't be anything his right-hand man Tony had done, or else he would have been forewarned of the situation. Plus, Tony was up in Memphis, Tennessee, tending to some much-needed family business back home. Besides, if anything of that nature meant Tony had crossed him somehow, no two regular town policemen would have shown up. Quan was big fish, and with that, the bigger boys would have apprehended him instead.

FBI. DEA. And they wouldn't just be in a cold room waiting to hear some bullshit. Quan would know his fate if it had been any of the Alphabet Boys involved. And right when the short hand hit five o'clock, the interrogation room door opened, and a light chuckle sounded from Quan.

Detective Bo Henderson was his name. This man was a hustler's nightmare, a killer, and a menace all at the same time. He and Quan had bumped heads numerous times over the years, but Bo could never catch Quan red-handed for nothing. However, Bo had a way to get under one's skin till a breaking point, and perhaps this was one of those trying moments of his. This was pretty much Detective Bo's house—whatever he said goes—and not even the Chief himself could tell him what to do. The man was hell if he had his own lawmen afraid of him, and he hadn't been behind the badge but seven years. Already, he was labeled the king of the jungle in his department.

"How ya' feelin', Quan?" said Bo, a man of average height and tough-looking. He had a long scar slanted down the side of his face, resulting from a childhood incident after climbing a pecan tree.

"I'm cool," Quan shrugged.

"Cool." Bo took a seat across from Quan, and to his surprise, he pulled a blunt from his shirt pocket and lit it up.

All Quan could do was shake his head. In all the years he'd visited this same interrogation room, he had never witnessed the actions the detective was presenting right now. The man was a nutcase, but vicious too.

"You know why you're here, Quan?"

No answer.

"The murder of Prince St. James about four weeks ago," said Detective Bo, puffing on the potent weed as its smoke filled the room. "Killed execution style in the office of his own nightclub around the way. And guess what? You left your calling card behind that no one recognized except for me, homeboy," he replied.

Still, Quan did not say a thing.

"Wanna know what that calling card was?" Bo said, and offered Quan the blunt.

He sneered at the detective like a vicious hyena thirsty for blood. Then Bo reached into the pocket of his windbreaker and produced a beaded bracelet. The beads were black and gold—Quan's two favorite colors—and its inscription, "Tia

N Daddy," was spelled out along the circular band of beads. Bo set the bracelet on the table before them and snickered over at Quan.

If anybody had willpower as strong as steel, it was Quan. He stared down at the bracelet as a bubble of emotions swelled up in him. He knew that very same bracelet. It belonged to his dead daughter, Tia Renee. After the sickle cell disease claimed her young life, that was the only possession of his daughter that he cherished dearly. Tia had loved that bracelet. He remembered the day she made it. The memory of it made his heart squeeze with a deep pain he would never rid himself of. Since her death two and a half years ago, Quan had carried that bracelet around in his pocket every day.

Until five weeks ago, when he damn near lost his mind at its disappearance—and sure enough, it was declared missing the night after he met with Prince in his club office. The very same night they shook hands to seal a deal they agreed on, and Quan left the office with him smiling that crooked smile of his.

"Some shit just don't make no sense, huh, Quan?" said Bo, smiling wickedly across the table.

Quan broke and reached for the bracelet and secured it into the fist of his hand.

"Took you long enough."

Quan was staring at his tight fist, then lifted his gaze up to look at Bo.

"Feel like talkin' now, homeboy?"

Quan nodded. "Yeah."

Bo smoked his blunt and leaned back in his chair.

"A'ight. Talk to me straight."

"Okay," Quan replied.

Then he hawked up some cold phlegm and spat it across at Bo, hitting him square in the face with it.

"Suck my dick, you pussy ass, mark ass nigga!" he retorted.

Bo said, "You nasty muthafucker."

Quan just smirked. Then he lunged across the table at him.

***

Her name was Daisy, and to the hood she was a sweetheart but a little rough around the edges too. Daisy had just pulled up to a stop at the corner of Hamilton Street in her Dodge Chrysler to answer her ringing phone. Suddenly, the passenger door opened and in slid Zion into the seat next to her. Startled by the sudden action, Daisy dropped her phone and was about to bolt until he stopped her.

"No. It's me. It's okay," said Zion, taking ahold of her arm. "Sorry I scared you."

"Zee," she said, placing a hand over her heart.

"I need your help, Daisy."

She swallowed. "Okay. You scared me, boy! Don't ever do that again."

"Promise," he swore.

Then Zion slid very low into his seat to prevent anyone from seeing him. Although he was pretty certain someone had witnessed him get into the car with her, he just hoped that someone didn't ring the alarm to the bad boys. Seeing this, Daisy automatically knew he was in trouble, especially with the bruised cheek and his busted lip.

"Somebody tryna kill me," he said.

"Who?"

"Will you please just drive, Daisy. Please just get me away from here," he pleaded with her as she drove on, having forgotten all about the phone in her lap.

Once they had gotten onto Martin L. King Blvd. and were heading north, it was then that Zion risked lifting his head up to peer outside.

"Why are somebody tryna kill you, Zee? From my understandin', you don't mess wit' nobody. I must say, you're one of the good ones we got around here," she told him.

"Thanks for the confidence," he said.

"Why, Zee?"

He didn't answer right away.

"I'm picking up Lana from her track meet and takin' her to Tallahassee. Where do you want me to take you, Zee?"

He thought about twelve-year-old Lana and knew there was no way he would jeopardize her life if he stayed with them.

"Take me to my cousin Sheena's house," said Zion, knowing that he would be a whole lot safer with her.

There he would contact Oscar, and together they'd figure this mess out. Daisy knew exactly where Sheena lived but said that she wanted to pick up Lana first. Of course, he wanted to tell her no, but who was he to demand what she did in her life?

"Okay," he said.

Lana was conducting her track meet over at James A. Shanks Middle School, which was formerly a high school before East Gadsden High was built years ago. That was when Shanks was the talk of the town, undefeated in all sports and having even molded several professional athletes.

Ten minutes later, the Chrysler pulled into the entrance of the school's wide parking lot, then onward to where the school's track field was located near the rear of the lot. Lana was already waiting amidst her two favorite teammates, Ashlee and Megan. For a twelve-year-old, Lana was tall—almost five foot nine—and yet still growing. When she saw her big sister's car, Lana hugged her friends and picked up her gym bag.

Zion then got out of the car so that Lana could have the front seat, and that was yet another mistake for him, having never gotten out of the car where he could be identified. It just so happened someone who had come to retrieve their loved one, waiting behind the wheel of their car, saw him.

By this time, Zion's name had been making its rounds through the street channels. The nigga was going viral without even knowing, but that same attention was dangerous for him.

"What's up, Zee!" Lana greeted him after offering him one of her bottles of Gatorade.

He accepted it and popped the top immediately.

"Oh, didn't I mention Lana was accepted to join the Junior Olympics this coming fall? Yeah. Baby gurl is doing the damn thang," said Daisy, praising her little sister.

"How fast are you now, Lana?" he asked.

The girl glanced back at him with the prettiest dark brown eyes.

"Today I ran a four-seven in the forty," she boasted.

"What!" Zion was impressed by those numbers.

That's when he tossed caution to the wind and rewarded her with two hundred dollars. He then told her that in order to run her best, she had to be running in the best cleats too. Lana all but cried her thanksgiving. He was proud of her, but yet he was also scared too.

Chapter 8

When the Chevy Tahoe pulled into the entrance of the Golden Falcon gas station, Prep stepped from alongside the building and opened the passenger door to get inside. In the back seat, Yvonnie gripped her pistol tightly, knowing her unexpected presence was about to alarm Prep greatly.

"Oh shit! Yvonnie . . ." Prep gasped when he glanced back and saw her sitting behind him with this menacing smirk on her face.

"Where is the rest of your crew, Prep?" she questioned, grateful that Block had informed her in advance after receiving the call from Prep to come scoop him up.

"They gone, Yvonnie," Prep said.

"Gone."

He went into account what transpired after they received a tip from Loony's little brother about where they could find Zion.

"So you still didn't recover the bag, I see," Yvonnie sounded so disappointed.

He went on to explain how Oscar and Sheena pulled up on the scene and killed everybody before he had to get out of Dodge.

"You ran away, nigga?" Block cut in.

Prep shifted in his seat.

"I had no choice, my nigga. Shit was getting—"

Suddenly, his brains exploded through the front of his head from the bullet Yvonnie put there into the back of his cranium.

This action astounded Block so much that he almost wrecked the truck. Some of the blood had splattered along the side of his face as it sprayed the windshield and the dashboard in front of him. Then Yvonnie leaned over the seat and dumped two more slugs into Prep's back. She was mad, and Prep pissed her off even more.

"This bitch Sheena done got beside herself now," Yvonnie hissed. "She got to get it now, too."

"Who is Oscar?" Block asked.

"He's Zion's homeboy. They're supposed to be like brothaz or something."

"So it's fair game wit' him too?"

"Fair game."

Block needed to ditch the truck because Prep's dead body was going to raise all kinds of hell. So he dropped Yvonnie off on St. John Road near where she left her Jeep after putting Quan's car away at his duck-off spot in the country area.

Once she reclaimed her car, Yvonnie received the phone call she'd been waiting on—the call that was surely going to make Zion hurt. So much so that he would have no choice but to cough the money up, or else his mother would die. Painfully.

"Tell me something good, Dray."

"Got Mama Bear secured," he replied.

Just hearing those words made Yvonnie want to scream out in joy. If only Quan knew the hell she was causing out there in the streets to honor him and the life of his mother.

Dray said, "I'm on my way to that spot where Lil Murda got his teeth knocked out," meaning he was headed to Scott Town, which was where Dray was originally from.

"I'm already close by right now," Yvonnie said, looking for a spot to turn around and head out to Scott Town way.

Getting there from St. John would be a quick drive. Now that she had Zion's mother, there shouldn't be no problem getting the money now. Plus, Zion wasn't no real dog, so the pressure she was about to apply would break him.

But Sheena was, thought Yvonnie with dismay.

If she had anything to do with it, then things were bound to get even more interesting. You had to be careful with Sheena. Can't sleep on her. The bitch was literally bred for this gangster shit they were about to put down.

***

Hazel wasn't getting up no time soon. The heavy dose of pain meds gonna have her in a slumber for a while. Which was all the well with Rashia, but still, she was having a hard time accepting what's happened.

Another heart attack, thought Rashia miserably.

This time Rashia wasn't there, and what if she had lost Hazel this time? That would have killed Rashia. Just the thought of her dying made her sick.

While sitting at her grandmother's bedside, holding one of her hands in her own, Rashia's saddened thoughts of losing her were interrupted by the opening of the room door. That's when Kiarah entered, and Rashia felt her heart burn with emotion.

This was Rashia's best friend, Kiarah, the niece of a thoroughbred goon by the name of Moby. Speaking of which, that's exactly who walked through the door behind her next. Moby was an older, slim, brown-skinned nigga who favored the rapper Snoop Dogg, and a dog he was. Plus, he bites hard, and Moby had no problem shedding blood for his respect.

Kiarah rushed to Hazel's bedside as Rashia rose up to place herself in her friend's arms.

"You don't look so good," said Kiarah, pointing out that Rashia had a busted lip and a darkening bruise along the side of her face.

She was of a high yellow skin tone complexion, which pronounced the bruise clearly upon her beautiful face.

"I know I do, sis."

"What happen?"

Moby exchanged eye contact with Rashia before she turned her gaze back on her friend. There was something in the fleeting of her gaze that told the gangsta a story of a young woman scorned. He saw death in her eyes.

In her mind, she was being told not to say anything, but her heart wouldn't allow her to look in Kiarah's eyes and tell her a lie.

"Rashia," Kiarah took her hand and squeezed it reassuringly. "You can talk to me. I know all about the kidnap," she said. "A friend of a friend called me and told me what they saw. That's why Uncle Moby is here wit' me. He needs to know so that he could get to the bottom of it."

Rashia shook her head and looked away.

"So you won't tell?" said Kiarah.

"No," Rashia replied. "It's not that, Kiarah. It's just so much had happened to me in the past two hours. I'm so scared right now," she cried.

"You was kidnapped," said Moby. "But what I'm tryna understand is why? And how did you manage to get away so fast?"

"Because I was the wrong person."

"Huh."

"Can you please elaborate on that for me, please?" Kiarah leaned against the bed and folded her arms over her perky breasts.

Reclaiming her seat next to the bed, Rashia sighed deeply and told them everything. She told them what she had gone through from the moment she received that phone call up until that very point. Although her story was severely affecting, Moby didn't press the issue when Rashia didn't name names. She was very specific about what went down, but Rashia had no clue how in debt she still was.

To hear her friend had to kill another human being in order to save herself sickened Kiarah. Then she looked over at her uncle in silent plea.

"And the gun you used to do it?" said Moby.

"I still have it," she said.

"Where is it?"

Hesitantly, Rashia got up and stepped over the hospital bed, where she retrieved the gun. When Kiarah saw the gun, she unfolded her arms and once again looked over to her uncle.

"Oh no," whispered Moby.

"What? You don't want it?" said Rashia.

"Donte."

"Um, what?" Rashia stiffened.

Moby reached for the gun and Rashia let him take it away from her. This was the same man who gave her as much of a father figure as one could offer. He couldn't take the place of her grandfather, Dean, who passed away almost five years ago. He had been her rock, her hero, but Moby had been something else entirely.

With the gun in his possession, Moby said, "This is a Walther P22 pistol, chrome plated with the red ruby handle. The only person I know in this world that owns a customized pistol like this is Donte Jones. How I know this is because my brotha Big Two sold it to him about a year ago."

"Uncle Two?" said Kiarah.

Moby looked at Rashia sternly.

"So it was Donte that had you kidnapped," he muttered.

She didn't answer.

"Don't worry," said Moby. "I'll handle it from here," he added before motioning to conceal the weapon.

"No!" Rashia quickly reached out to grab ahold of his wrist.

Then she relieved him of the gun and re-tucked it at her waistline.

“This is mine now, Uncle Moby. It’s staying wit’ me from now on.”

“Suit yourself,” he said.

“And don’t say nothing about this.”

“I’m not sure I can do that, Rashia. He had you hurt and that’s unacceptable in my book.”

“He spared my life too, Unc.”

He frowned.

“I got this,” Rashia told him. “I got Donte,” she said, and meant every single word.

Chapter 9

As usual, Shaw Quarters was buzzing with activity when the Chrysler rolled through the set. Zion stared out his side window in passing as he surveyed the area before him. He couldn't wait to finally link up with his cousin Sheena. He knew she was street royalty and could get shit done accordingly.

A couple minutes later, the car swerved over along the curb outside a white and beige-colored house with the big fenced-in front yard. Parked outside in the driveway before the two-car garage was Sheena's pearl-white Ferrari 296 GTB and her 1100 Yamaha Hayabusa street bike. In the garage, Zion knew, sat a mint-condition '64 Impala—candy apple green and 28-inch chrome floaters to slide in. It was just a show car that Sheena only brought out every now and then, just to change the game for a minute.

"Thanks, Daisy," said Zion, opening the door and about to get out.

"Zee?" Lana called after him.

He glanced over at the girl.

"Be careful," she said, and Zion noticed that her pretty brown eyes were serious. "You're the golden child. Everythang's gonna be okay."

"I hope so, Lana." He bumped fists with her and got out of the car.

He saluted Daisy and proceeded to let himself in through the front gate. In passing, Zion noticed old man Mr. Willie sitting out on his front porch next door, rocking in his outside chair while listening to his oldie goldies. Two young boys rode past on their bicycles, laughing as they raced up the street. Behind him, across the street, were Trevor and Lucci—two of Sheena's homeboys that Zion knew well from his occasional visits.

He followed the stone path up to the front door of the house and knocked.

"Diamond," said Zion when he heard Sheena's dog let out a bark in response.

Diamond was a gray and white bulldog that Sheena had had for about five years now. Good thing Diamond and Zion had a good relationship, or else he would've been torn to pieces a long time ago.

Zion thought about his beef with Shocker earlier and knew if given the opportunity, Diamond would make him her bitch. She was one stubborn bitch herself. Diamond was a killer. Sheena had told him the story in regards to siccing Diamond on one of her archenemies, and she ripped his throat out on command. Her and Sheena were two of the same.

The front door opened—but it wasn't Sheena who stood before him. It was her wifey, Lyric, who was suddenly nudged aside by Diamond, who came out to greet him humbly.

"Get in here," said Lyric. "Quickly!" She took him by the arm and pulled him through the door.

"Where is Sheena?" he asked.

"She's out there lookin' for you, Zion. But rest assured, we're about to call her right now," Lyric told him as she led the way into the spacious living room where she was in the process of chasing her drink with grapefruit juice.

Zion followed behind her, trying not to stare at her 42-inch ass bouncing like crazy in the pink and white boy-shorts she was wearing. When he took a seat upon the plush recliner to rest his nerves, Diamond came over and laid down at his feet. Zion reached down to stroke her head, then removed the backpack.

"Is it really true what they're saying you did to Quan?" asked Lyric.

"No."

"Then what's wit' all that bullshit?"

He sighed. "I'm only doing what Quan asked me to do," he told her. "And that's protect this bag no matter what." He lifted the bag up in the air.

"So what's in the bag, then?"

"A whole bunch of money." Zion didn't have no problem telling her the truth.

Lyric was not only loyal to his cousin, but him too—for she had already proven that to him twice before. For a moment, Lyric didn't respond as she sat nursing her drink. The central air blowing throughout the house was a great relief to Zion, as he suddenly felt lazy for some reason.

"Okay," she said. "C'mere. Follow me."

Lyric got back up and beckoned Zion down the nearby hall, where she then led him into Sheena's home study. Zion was clutching the money bag for dear life as he watched Lyric activate the digital wall safe behind the seven-foot bookshelf near the desk. When its door swung open, Zion gasped at the contents he saw inside the large safe.

"Gimme the bag so I can store it in here?"

He shook his head no.

"It'll be safer in here than you carrying it around all over the place." She tried to reason with him, and the look Zion gave her was graveyard serious.

"You don't trust me?"

"It's not about that, Lyric."

"Then what is it about? Because I can—"

Zion cut her off, and Lyric stopped talking.

"Please, Lyric. Don't waste your time. This bag ain't leaving my sight. People died today behind this money, and I'm not lettin' it go."

To punctuate his point, Zion drew his Beretta and turned away from Lyric to leave the room. He was given a mission that he must honor. No matter what. Not even Sheena could change that.

***

Dray grew up in the country area of Scott Town, on farmland. His grandparents were farmers. They made a living raising livestock—cows, goats, and chickens—to keep them busy on a daily basis. The land had been pretty much run down since the death of his grandparents. The livestock dwindled down to nothing, leaving the farm yearning for something other than an old barn.

Speaking of which, the old barn was where shit be going down at. From group meetings to hangouts, and now—the prison where Dray had Zion's mother bound and gagged. When Yvonnie arrived on the scene, she already knew where to find the action.

"Did she make it hard for you?" asked Yvonnie after gaining entrance into the old barn.

She had to walk out to his location from the house, which was about two hundred yards out. Present were Dray, Trent, and Poochie—all armed with heavy artillery and seriously about that issue when it was called for.

"It wasn't, when Poochie got involved. You know that bitch can talk the teeth outta a lion's mouth," said Dray with a smirk.

Yvonnie looked over at the other female and nodded at her respectfully.

"She over here," said Dray, waving for Yvonnie to follow him.

He led her to one of the stalls, which was cluttered with whatnots and an old broken-down wheelbarrow. That's where she was—hog-tied and gagged, with duct tape sealing her mouth shut. When Yvonnie entered the stall and came to rest before Tabitha Williams, she glared down at the woman with fire in her eyes.

"You just don't know how bad we need your cooperation right now, Tabitha," said Yvonnie.

The look Zion's mother gave her in return was all the indication Yvonnie needed to scowl and draw her gun. Even at the sight of the gun, Tabitha didn't switch up her evil stare that unnerved Yvonnie.

Regardless of the fact that she was at their mercy, Zion's mother knew what was to become of her. She had overheard the others talking about her son. She was willing to endure whatever they had in mind for her. Tabitha still wasn't gonna give up her son. If Yvonnie thought she would get her cooperation, then she had another thing coming.

"Then again," said Yvonnie, "all you gotta do is stay put and look pretty. Your cooperation isn't needed at all—just your body."

Then she turned to Trent and told him to let her borrow his phone.

"Sorry, Yvonnie, but my phone broke two days ago," said Trent with an apologetic shrug.

"All that money you makin' and you can't buy another damn phone?" Yvonnie said with attitude, and accepted the one offered by Poochie.

She then took two pictures of Tabitha with the phone, one of them being with a gun to her head.

"Now let's see what we get in return," she replied.

"Which means we got a number to reach him?"

"Not exactly, Dray," Yvonnie told him. "But I'm gonna improvise the matter by calling the only other person besides Zion's best friend Oscar—and that's his cousin Sheena."

"Sheena?" said Trent. "Are you talkin' about Sheena Jones or Sheena Smith?"

There were two known women in town by the name of Sheena, and one of them in particular was a stone-cold murderer by trade.

"I'm talkin' about Sheena Smith."

Instantly, Dray and Poochie looked at each other and shook their heads. Seeing the effect Sheena had on them, Yvonnie removed herself from their sight, walking back toward the front of the barn. Then she placed the call in through to Sheena. Even dialing her number now gave her goosebumps. Being an enemy of hers wasn't good. It was suicidal.

"Hello?" came Sheena's voice on the second ring, and Yvonnie braced herself.

"So how are we gonna play this, Sheena?" said Yvonnie after forwarding the pictures to her phone. "All I want is that money bag that Zion has. Wit' everythang that came in it—or else his mama dies."

"Is that all you got?"

Yvonnie heard the malice in her voice. Right then, the phone in Yvonnie's hand vibrated with an incoming video call.

"Answer the phone, Yvonnie," chuckled Sheena in that devilish way she does. "I got something I wanna show you too," she said.

A sense of trepidation washed over Yvonnie at that moment, feeling whatever it was—just a click away—might do her in. She switched over to the video call, and that's when she got the shock of her life. Yvonnie almost dropped the phone when she recognized the woman who was at Sheena's feet—her very own grandmother. And not only that—there was her eight-year-old niece Makayla, and Yvonnie's beloved sister Jill as well. They all were lying face down with their arms zip-tied behind them.

"You wanna reconsider what you're doing now, bitch?" said Sheena aggressively. "You touch one of mines, so I touched three of yours."

Yvonnie closed her eyes, as if she could block out the images that were now branded in her brain. It threatened to make her cry—even.

"You see, Yvonnie . . . I know you well. I know how bitches like you think. You can't catch Zee, so you took his mama. But I got news for you, Yvonnie." Sheena was staring into the camera of the phone as she stood among the three captives. "Your best-friend sista, Felix—yeah, she's on the way too."

"Let my people go, Sheena. They don't got nothing to do with this."

"And neither does my auntie," retorted Sheena. "So what's it gonna be? Then again, I already know what it is. Have my auntie free and unharmed in the next ten minutes when I call back. You know the drill, bitch."

The line was disconnected.

"No . . ." Yvonnie whimpered.

She turned back for the stall where Tabitha was and glared down at the woman with a silent hatred in her heart. She almost made the mistake of shooting her in the face. What looked like a smirk formed beyond the gag on Tabitha's face.

"You are so lucky, bitch," she sneered.

Yvonnie felt so fuckin' stupid after having just been beat at her own game. It was depressing.

Chapter 10

The car was dead silent as Donte stared out his side window while they rode through traffic. Killah looked over at his road dawg and could see that he was worried about something—so caught up in whatever it was that Donte wasn't even paying attention to him. This was perhaps the richest nigga in the game right now, and here he was lookin' like he'd lost his best friend or something.

A man of his status shouldn't have no worries when he had everything he ever wanted. At thirty-two years old, Donte was so accomplished in the street game that he could literally buy his small town. He had everything a gangsta could ever hope for—in the name of money, power, and respect. He was blessed with measure. Donte was a charm.

He also was a two-time felon who'd done a short prison bid for felony battery against the county commissioner. That was his way of taking one for the team of Quincy, and his people applauded him for it. Then he utilized his time behind the wall to study the game of finance and investment. He went from investing in Bitcoin and takin' up stocks to investing his earnings into street hustles from right there in his prison cell. Five years later, Donte was released from prison with four legitimate businesses and a nice bank account to be proud of.

Fast forward three years later, and now Donte had the whole town in the palm of his hand. But he didn't live in Quincy no more because his status wouldn't allow him to do so. He was content with his life; he did what he could to please his people. Regardless of where his foot was in the game, Donte still stepped in the trenches. He didn't forget where he came from. There were only a few who shared the same perspectives as him—and one of them was his longtime crime partner, Quan.

Quan was upset with him after not showin' up for his birthday bash a month ago. Quan had leased out the whole Civic Center in Tallahassee for the weekend. Some big names were present in the building, but none of them mattered as much as it would've if Donte had been there. During that time, Donte was too preoccupied with the business of trying to save his godfather, Larry Dempson.

He was the focal point of why Rashia had been kidnapped earlier. She'd been mistaken for Valerie Schultz, the star witness to the murder of her uncle Johnathan Schultz—the murder she claimed Larry committed. John Schultz was leaving his private medical firm one evening when he was stabbed to death in the parking lot. It just so happened Valerie was there waiting to retrieve him. It took Donte a while to learn the name of the witness, and now that he knew, the universe was makin' it hard for him to capture her.

Valerie was a slippery one to catch. It was like she knew what was coming. All Donte had to go on was her identity and the model car she drove. Valerie purposely stayed away from her Midway residence and avoided interaction with friends and family. Her moment to testify at trial against Donte's godfather was four weeks away, and she knew better than to get caught slippin'. The bitch was smart. She was careful not to be seen.

Until it was crunch time. And even then, Valerie would still play her position accordingly. All she wanted was to avenge her uncle's death by making sure the man responsible got hanged for it. And that's where Donte was right now—trying to do whatever he could to save his godfather. The same man who gave him hope when Donte felt like there was no hope left to give. Larry was a great man to him. He was the best.

"Rashia," muttered Donte after wallowing in silence since they left the garage.

"What? Who?" Killah glanced over at Donte to find him sitting upright in his seat.

"I know her now," said Donte. "I knew she looked familiar. A man could never forget those eyes. Rashia. She works at *Crowns Hair and Nail Salon*, where I got my cousin Trina managing."

"Brah?"

"Yeah."

"All this time you been givin' me the silent treatment is 'cause you been thinkin' about a bitch?" said Killah with a frown.

Donte didn't reply.

"You in love wit' her," Killah replied. "I can see that shit in your eyes."

"Bullshit."

"You can't front with me, my nigga. You my muthafuckin' brotha. I know what I'm seein'. You saw that young bad, pretty-eyed bitch put in that work earlier, and now you got the blues."

Donte shook his head wearily. "You so wrong, Killah. It ain't even like that at all."

"Bullshit. You in love. Only a nigga who don't know better can't see that shit." Killah laughed out loud. "Sucker-ass nigga sittin' here with little hearts in his eyes for a bitch."

"But there's somethin' about her though," Donte said, looking at him.

"What?"

"The way she handled that shit today. It was like she was in a zone or somethin'."

"Yeah. She was. After killin' that nigga Moon, she knew she had to do somethin' to convince you she didn't wanna be next."

"Nah, brah, she done killed before. She ain't new to this shit. I want you to find out all you can about her. Where she come from. Who her people are." Donte scratched his bald head.

"The full report. I gotcha, brah."

Right then, Donte's phone rang, and he fished it from the pocket of his slacks to check who was callin'. When he saw Mario Peteld's number, he answered it. Mario was his confidential source—whose information Donte valued greatly. In all the years they'd known each other, Mario hadn't disappointed him yet.

"Quan was taken into custody not too long ago."

Donte shifted in his seat.

"What for?"

"Apparently issues with Bo, 'cause that's who got him in the room right now. But it gets deeper than that, Donte. Before takin' him in, Quan was rollin' with young Zion Griffen. The boy jumped out and took off before anyone could get him."

"Okay," Donte said, sensing there was more coming.

"Somehow it's gotten out that Zion played a part in Quan being apprehended," said Mario.

Then he went on to explain how Yvonnie was callin' the shots now and wreakin' havoc all over town in her desperate need to capture Zion.

"A total of seven people done died behind this mess already, and I believe more will be coming before the day is out."

"Who're the ones that died?"

Mario gave up the names, and Donte literally felt his blood pressure go up. He knew Prep, Rocko, Trill, and young MiMi Rogers. Her big brother, Meat Rogers, was one of his money runners. As for the others, Donte could only hope their deaths didn't affect anyone he cared for personally.

"I'll look into it," said Donte. "But keep me posted on Quan's situation, though."

"Without a doubt."

After sharing a few more things, Donte disconnected with Mario and leaned his head back, closing his eyes for a moment.

"Yvonnie is doin' too much right now."

"She is," agreed Donte.

"Want me to hit her up?"

What Donte really wanted was somethin' cold to drink—and he told him so.

"This whole situation is about to blow up into somethin' big, Killah," said Donte. "I got love for Yvonnie 'cause she my brotha's wife. But Sheena is my heart—and bein' that Zion is her cousin, she liable to do so much damage that Quan will be forced to go after her."

"That won't be good."

"It won't."

The car turned into the entrance of the 24-hour Kelly Jr. gas station downtown. Killah eased the big car into the available parking space near the door's entrance and killed the ignition.

"You believe the lil' nigga played a part in Quan gettin' snatched up?"

"Hell no," said Donte. "Whatever happened, the situation is blown outta proportion to the point Yvonnie only saw a threat to her love life and her livelihood—and was doin' what she felt was probable."

"So what you gonna do?"

Donte said, "I don't know, brah."

Then he opened his side door, exited the car, and went inside the store with clouded thoughts.

Can I put an end to this nonsense? he wondered.

***

Hank had eventually made it back to the hospital after going back to the house to lock it up because of the time he'd vowed to spend watching over Hazel. Rashia loved him for that and had told him so.

In return, Hank had brought back the clothes Rashia had asked him to retain for her and Hazel. He was right on time. Meanwhile, Rashia was occupying the adjoining bathroom with Kiarah as they talked and she changed into fresh clothes.

"I gotta go check Trina's ass when or if Uncle Moby comes back with my car. That bitch just disrespected the fuck outta me on the phone."

"About what?"

"When I called to inform her on my family emergency, the bitch spazzed out on me," said Rashia, stepping into her fitted jeans. "She was yellin' all in my ear talkin' about I had two scheduled appointments this afternoon, and if I can't show up for work, I might as well don't ever show up at all."

"So she fired you?" Kiarah said.

Rashia was seething. "I'ma show her tired ass today," she replied. "You don't disrespect my shit and think I won't test that ass."

"Oh trust me, I know."

Kiarah and her had been good friends since the seventh grade, when Kiarah moved just across the street from her. She'd seen Rashia at her worst and had witnessed her during her darkest hours. If there was one person who knew Rashia, it was Kiarah. They were sistas. Their love and loyalty to one another was something to be admired.

When Rashia called Kiarah earlier, Kiarah was at work tending to her shoppers at the local Super Walmart shopping center. Kiarah didn't even hesitate phoning her uncle to come get her so she could be with her girl. It was also during that time when Kiarah was struck with the news of Rashia being kidnapped. It reminded her how dangerous the town was compared to some of the other spots.

"I'ma deal with Trina alone too, Kiarah. I don't need you behind me on this one."

"You're gonna shoot her too?" she asked.

"I just might."

"Rashia."

She looked at her friend.

"I'm not playin'. That heifer gets my timing wrong and I'ma put a slug in her fat ass."

Moby eventually showed back up with her car keys in hand—and a police investigator wanting to question her about the incident. Of course, Rashia had nothing to tell them besides she was alive and well.

"Don't push," Moby warned the investigator menacingly when the white man attempted to demand information from her that she chose not to give.

The investigator left the room fuming mad, having just wasted his precious time. Not long after the investigator took his leave, Rashia kissed her grandmother's rosy cheek and hit the door with Kiarah and Uncle Moby in tow. Once again, she told Kiarah to not get involved with what she was about to do.

"Just be careful and watch your back," Moby told her after being explained the situation. "Your grandma needs you."

"Sure she does—"

Rashia and her crew were near the exit doors when all of a sudden a team of paramedics rushed inside from the ER's entrance to their right. They had someone on a gurney, and it wasn't looking so good with all the blood and stuff.

"Oh my God! I know that girl," said Rashia when they raced past them, headed to the ER as fast as their feet would allow.

"Who is she?" asked Kiarah.

Rashia was also staring after the female who was hurrying alongside the gurney, crying, and telling her loved one to hold on and be strong. The scene was so moving that Rashia felt an emotional shudder pass through her.

"Rashia?"

"Excuse me." Moby broke away from them and headed in the same direction as the team of paramedics and the severely injured girl.

"Now where is he going?" wondered Kiarah as she and Rashia watched him hurry away.

"I don't know," said Rashia. "But I know where I'm going. Love you, sis."

"Love you too. But you said you know that girl they just rushed in here?"

Together, the two of them exited the doors outside, where the sun was creating a furnace.

"She's one of the regulars at the shop. A sweet little girl. Very pretty and humble. Now somebody done shot her up, fuckin' up her life, and shit like that irks the fuck outta me."

"Rashia." Kiarah took her friend by the arm when she sensed Rashia losing herself in the moment. "That was fifteen years ago. You've been doing so well. Don't let what you just saw be the reason you go out there and go off the deep end like you did before," she said.

"Look at this shit, Kay!" Rashia lifted up her shirt to reveal two old gunshot wounds to her stomach area. "I'll never forget what they did to me that night. But I got it, baby. I won't let it rule over my life like I let it do all those years ago."

"Please."

Rashia hugged her friend and kissed her on the forehead. Then she turned away to go in search of her car. Kiarah didn't go after her. She just watched her leave in silence.

Silence—that's what it's not going to be when Rashia reached her destination. She was about to get live and affect.

Chapter 11

For a second, Zion thought Lyric was about to get on some other shit, but then she called Sheena and put him on the phone with her. That's when Sheena dropped that bomb on him about his mother.

Lyric saw something awaken in Zion when he learned about his mother being kidnapped. He had ran for the door in an attempt to go out and try to save her, but then he stopped in the doorway after realizing he wouldn't know where to start in finding her.

It was when Oscar got on the phone next and Zion was encouraged to calm down that inner beast in him. Oscar knew just the right words to say to put him at ease, but just knowing his mother had been taken against her will was maddening. Now, for the past ten minutes since hanging up with his brother from another mother, Zion had been out back chillin' on the porch, watching Diamond at play in the backyard.

It wasn't long before the back door of the neighbor's residence opened, and an older female stepped outside with her laundry basket. She looked to be in her mid-forties, not all that good-looking but with one helluva body. If he's not mistaken, Zion would guess her name was Pumpkin. He remembered her having a son about his age—a real mellow kid who played the trumpet in the school band. Zion wasn't too sure about him, but what he did know was the kid was a loner. He didn't run the streets, didn't talk much from Zion's observation of him at school. So there shouldn't be nothin' to worry about with him.

Zion needed this time alone to rest and clear his thoughts.

Then the back door opened, and Lyric peeped her head out to tell him that she was about to leave for the store.

"You want me to bring you anything back?" she asked him kindly.

"All I want is my mama and for all this bullshit to end, Lyric."

She nodded her understanding.

After taking her leave, Zion waited another minute or two before calling for Diamond. The dog turned on command and approached Zion to follow him back into the house. He entered the front room, where he stepped before the living room window and pulled the curtains aside.

About five seconds too late, he would've missed the movement of two armed goons hurrying along either side of the house.

Zion instantly took a step back from the window as he realized what was actually taking place.

They were outside the house.

Zion drew his weapon and dashed for the hallway. Then he stopped in the middle of the hallway. He waited. Zion pressed his back against the wall. Then he listened.

His heart was beating so hard, it was a wonder they didn't hear it outside.

There was nothing. No kicking in the door with guns blazing. Nothing whatsoever.

That's when it finally hit him.

The two goons running around back . . .

They had come for him because he had been out back on the porch. An easy shot at the money.

"Lyric," muttered Zion, with disdain for what he knew she had done.

No one knew he was back there but Lyric. Then she used going to the store as an excuse to get away while the two goons handled him.

"Muthafucker," he said.

Apparently, the two goons didn't find him back there and went on about their business.

After holding his position another couple of minutes or so, Zion removed himself from the hallway to go wait on Lyric's return.

She had set him up for the kill.

Bad move.

Whoever the two goons were knew better than to come looking for him inside the house. That was a danger of its own, and it had nothing to do with Diamond or his Beretta.

They would be entering Sheena's home—which would have her hunting their ass down and delivering to them a very slow death. It also pretty much went hand-in-hand if they had succeeded with him out back. Sheena would not rest until she sought vengeance.

Those two niggas had to be stupid to allow themselves to be sent on a suicide mission.

Lyric walked through the door minutes later, carrying a bag of goodies.

When she saw him perched on the arm of the sofa, Zion caught the astounded reaction from her that he was looking for.

"You alright, Zee? I brought you something to drink and a snack cake, anyway."

Zion lifted up off the sofa and brought the Beretta up to aim it at her face.

"You thought you were so slick," he hissed.

"Huh? What're you talkin' about, Zion?"

Blocka!

That's what he was talking about.

***

Camillah Chambers was so mad she wanted to tear the whole house down—meaning make the whole entire Quinby Police Station feel her darkest wrath like never before. Detective Bo Henderson specifically. She wanted to kill him, literally.

"Make this the last time I have to come save your black ass here, Quan."

Quan pushed open the exit door of the police station.

"It ain't like I wanted to come here," he responded gruffly.

"Anywhere else, I'll be there—but back there . . ."

She hooked a thumb in the direction behind them.

"I hate those slimy assholes."

"Me too."

The confrontation between Quan and Detective Bo resulted in Quan sporting a black eye, bruised ribs, and a ringing in his right ear. Though one-handed, Quan had gotten a few good licks in himself. He had been far from intimidated by the detective—and had to show him that today.

Through it all, Quan still managed to make it out with his daughter's bracelet.

As for Bo, he didn't have long to breathe now. It was already sold to Quan's heart that he would kill the big bad detective once and for all. He would be doing the streets a huge favor by taking the man out the game.

Bo had to get dealt with accordingly.

His time was coming.

"Get in the truck, Quan."

Camillah pressed the button on her key fob to automatically unlock the doors to her Jeep Wagoneer.

She was pissed—and it wasn't good to piss her off. The woman was dangerous.

Camillah was a high-power attorney who handled the likes of street players and those of the elite group, but mainly she dealt personally with Donte; for if it wasn't for him, she would be working at the local seamstress shop.

For about four years now, Quan's unfortunate street affairs had had Camillah called up to bond him out of his troubles. They had a love-hate relationship that not even Donte would dare come in between of.

Quan got into the truck, and then they were in traffic, putting distance between them and the crooked police station.

"Where's your phone?" he asked.

"Not until you hear what I gotta say first, Quan. You really need to hear this now," Camillah told him, her tone serious—and Quan knew there was something bad about to be revealed.

"Okay," he stretched the word.

"It's about Yvonnie," she said. "Your wife."

Quan remained humbled.

"What about her?"

Last he'd known, Yvonnie was left back at the house before he headed out to go see the people who was going to save his mother's life.

Camillah told him about the abduction of Yvonnie's family in retaliation for the capture of Zion Griffen. At hearing this, Quan went into a panic and patted the woman's body down while she drove, in search of her phone. Camillah shot out a hard elbow strike to his torso to get him away from her, but Quan still came away with her phone after locating it in her coat pocket.

"You're lucky you are—"

"Shut up," he told her as he dialed Yvonnie's phone number.

His heart was racing like crazy as he hoped for Yvonnie to answer.

Sure enough, she answered the phone on the fifth ring—but when she spoke, Quan could tell by the tone of her voice that she was emotionally troubled at that moment.

"What the fuck have you done, Yvonnie!" he breathed fire into the receiver.

"Quan? Oh baby, Quan! I sent for Camillah to check on you. Did she?"

"I'm riding with her now."

"Where are you?"

He thought about it for a second.

"I'm on my way home. Be there. I don't care what you are doing. Get to the muthafuckin' house," he said with coldness in his tone.

"Okay," she said.

"Now. Yvonnie," he growled.

"Okay."

When he disconnected with her, Quan then put a call in to reach Sheena. He had no doubt in his mind it was her who had Yvonnie's people taken earlier.

"That fuckin' bag," he muttered.

"What?"

Quan looked over at Camillah and knew that she had no clue about the money bag. She knew everything else—but not the truth behind why any of this was even happening.

Sheena wasn't picking up.

"Fuck!"

That really had him worried.

For the rest of the drive to his house, Quan had called Sheena a total of six times to no avail. Then, when he did finally reach his destination, Quan wasn't even surprised to find Yvonnie waiting out front for him.

After the truck pulled to a halt at the curb, Quan got out and marched directly toward the woman he loved dearly.

"Baby, I'm sorry," Yvonnie replied. "I fucked up, Quan. Like really bad."

Whop!

Quan slapped her so hard, Yvonnie spun on her feet and hit the ground. Then he stepped over her fallen body and entered the house with two things on his mind:

Murder. And saving Lil' Zy.

Chapter 12

The best decision Yvonnie could've made today was to order the release of Zion's mother—at the risk of trusting that Sheena would honor her word and release her family afterward. Tabitha was dropped off back in town. Then she ran for the nearest telephone, which she found at the REC Center across from Shanks football field. She called Sheena immediately—and that's where she found her.

Now safely in the company of Sheena and her beloved Oscar—who was dressed in somebody else's blood—she demanded to know what was going on with her son. Sheena only told what she knew of the situation, with Oscar filling in what he was having a hard time believing.

"Fifty thousand dollars!" Tabitha gasped.

"Yep," Sheena nodded. "The bitch put a fifty-thousand-dollar hit on Zee's head."

Hearing this made Oscar boil with rage, which is why he took it out on Yvonnie's family. He only spared the girl's life—Makayla—forcing her to watch him slaughter her great-grandmother and her own mother. The whole time, Oscar made it clear to the girl that it was her aunt Yvonnie's fault this was happening. Oscar left the poor girl traumatized.

"So what now?" asked Tabitha, still a bit shaken over all that had happened.

"We're taking you to him now, Auntie," Sheena told her.

This was her father's only sibling before he died years ago from drunk driving out in Tallahassee after the club.

Tabitha bent her head for a small prayer in thanks that her son was safe. She couldn't wait to pull Zion into her loving arms and rain kisses upon his handsome face.

Within no time, they made the drive to Shaw Quarters, and Sheena swung the car along the curb outside her home.

"I gotta clean up," said Oscar as he got out of the car and stepped over to open the door for his best friend's mother.

"I got what you need inside," said Sheena.

As she led the way to the front door, she heard Diamond barking like crazy from inside. To Sheena, it didn't sound normal. She knew her dog and its behavioral patterns like the back of her hand. So Sheena rushed forward when her sixth sense told her something wasn't right.

"What's wrong?" asked Tabitha.

Oscar followed suit and took off running after Sheena while drawing his gun. The front door was unlocked, and Sheena gained entrance into the house without faltering much in her step.

"No . . ." Sheena panicked when she found Lyric motionless on the living room floor with a bullet hole in her face. Lyric was dead.

"Zion!" Tabitha bellowed.

Oscar moved her aside to step around Lyric's body and check the rest of the house for his brother. Sheena knelt before her woman's body as silent tears spilled from her eyes. Then she rose up to her feet and left the room to occupy her home study office.

"Where is Zion?" asked Tabitha.

"He's gone," Oscar answered a minute later, after finding the rest of the house empty.

He was very disturbed about the whole situation.

"Where did Sheena go?"

Tabitha shrugged exhaustively. "Somewhere down the hall. I don't know. I just want my baby, Oscar. I want my son."

Never in his life had Oscar witnessed her so vulnerable. He just pulled her into his arms and held her for a long moment, then kissed her weary head before going in search of Sheena. He was on the verge of losing it entirely.

He found Sheena sitting behind the desk in her home study office before two computer screens. The look on her face as she stared into the screens was worrisome. Sheena was seeing a ghost. Dumbstruck.

"Zee killed Lyric," she said.

"What?" Oscar paused.

"Look at this." She offered a gesture for him to come stand next to her.

Tabitha appeared in the doorway and moved inside the room when Oscar beckoned her over.

"What's this?" Tabitha asked.

"I have top-level surveillance surrounding this house—outside and inside," she said.

"But why?" asked Tabitha.

"It comes with the lifestyle I have, Auntie. I'm a hired killer wit' connections to the underworld, and there's always somebody out there who'll do anything to take your place. So I'm equipped wit' everythang I need to keep me ahead of the game. Now watch."

Sheena rewound the video footage back to where Zion was out on the porch.

"He's exposing himself," said Oscar. "C'mon, brah."

"Watch," Sheena replied.

During the time Zion was out back, Lyric was inside making a phone call. She stepped out back to say something to Zion. Then she left out the front door—only for Zion to reenter the house afterward. Maybe he sensed it, or maybe it was pure luck that Zion spotted the two goons moving around the back of the house, hoping to find him.

"She set him up," said Oscar.

The telltale sign was clear when the only person who knew he was back there was Lyric.

“He knows,” said Tabitha, seeing her son now in a light that revealed him facing his own crucial reality.

Then there was the wait . . . and Lyric returned. Zion killed her where she stood and disappeared out the back door.

“You bitch.” Sheena pushed away from the desk and stood up. Then she drew her pistol and headed for the exit.

Both Oscar and Tabitha looked at each other, then followed Sheena up front, where she came to rest standing over Lyric’s body.

“You betrayed me,” Sheena said before aiming the gun down at Lyric’s already mangled face.

Oscar braced himself.

Boc! Boc! Boc! Boc! Boc!

Five shots to the head was a messy job—but to Sheena, it was her art. The portrait of a woman scorned.

***

Zion seriously didn’t know what to do, or who to even trust at that point. Back at the house, he really didn’t mean to shoot Lyric in the face. He wanted to scare her a little—put her in her place and let Sheena deal with her. But when the gun went off, it freaked him the fuck out. Just seeing Lyric’s face explode from the impact of a bullet was so surreal. It was frightening. So he ran.

Earlier, when he shot Trill, that was by pure instinct. He didn’t have time to think it through. All he knew was either shoot or get shot.

Now, as he penetrated through the community of Shaw Quarters—moving along the side streets and easing toward the Hillside area—Zion was convinced that the only place he would be safe was where no one expected him to be.

Then he saw *him*.

Zion couldn’t believe it. He was going into the neighborhood’s corner store. So he hurried over across into the parking area of the store and slipped into the Dodge Ram truck. Once inside the truck, Zion slid down into the seat and waited.

Nine minutes later, Coach Raymond Thomas exited from the store and made his way over to his truck. Coach Thomas was a very big man—tall and wide-bodied like a professional offensive tackle. This was one of Zion's favorite people—his middle school football coach and mentor. One of the few men in his life that Zion could actually say he had love for.

Upon opening the driver door of his truck and seeing Zion hunched down in his seat, the coach shook his head wearily and climbed up inside.

"Hey, Coach," said Zion, still hunched low in the seat and sweating profusely.

The coach didn't respond. He just started the truck up and got it moving. Then, once they were in traffic, that's when he finally spoke.

"You've been creating a lot of trouble for yourself today, Zion. Not only just for you but for all those who support you and love you," coach Thomas said with a heavy heart.

"I didn't do nothing wrong, Coach."

"I believe you," he said.

"You have to believe me. I was just walking home from school when I caught a ride with my homeboy Quan, and the police pulled him over with me in the car. Quan gave me something and asked me to protect it until we linked back up. I made it home after I jumped out the car and ran, but that didn't last long before a group of niggas with guns kicked in my front door and started shootin' at me. It's been a nonstop mission from that point on." Zion sat upright in his seat finally.

"What was it Quan gave you?"

Zion didn't answer.

“You’ve told me this much—it’s only fair that you give me the whole truth. If not for me, do it for Candice,” said the coach.

At hearing Candice’s name, it made Zion look at the coach in astonishment. Then it registered—the relationship between him and Candice. She was supposed to be something like a second cousin. He and her mother were close cousins; they actually went to school together.

But Candice is dead, Zion thought, with a burning emotion of that reality.

“Rest assured, Zion, she is not dead. That’s where I was going before you hopped into my truck on the sly.”

“To see Candice?”

The coach nodded. “Yep.”

Something very troubling clicked at that moment, where Zion was thinking back on the idea he had come to terms with earlier. The hospital. They would not expect to look for him there. Especially not where he intended to go once he got there.

“Okay,” said Zion. “Let’s go see Candice. Then you’ll get the full truth.”

Chapter 13

Crowns Hair & Nail Salon was busy with activity and buzzing with gossiping women getting their last-minute hookups done. For many women, this was the spot to be when you wanted to really get information and get jazzy all at the same time. *Crowns* was the number one salon in between Quincy and Tallahassee. It housed the best hairstylists and nail technicians. What was once a *Family Dollar* shopping center had been renovated into a top-notch hair salon.

The place was live with talk and laughter until the entrance door opened, and Rashia stepped inside the building. Every mouth in the room was shut. Rashia scanned the room and didn't see who she came there for. There was only one other place she could be if she was anywhere in the building: in the back, occupying her office. Trina spent most of her time back there on the phone, or on the computer, or just entertaining guests she would have stop by the shop to hang out.

Drawing the chrome pistol amongst the group sent a series of gasps and nervous shifting in seats from the others. Then she pressed forward, moving in the direction of the rear of the building where the manager's office was.

"No, Rashia," said one of the stylists who suddenly abandoned her chair to come step into Rashia's path to block her. "You need to think about this, little sista. It's not even worth it, gurl."

"Move outta my way, Tiffany."

"Please, Rashia," she begged. "Don't do this."

Gripping the handle of the pistol tighter, Rashia glared into the woman's eyes. Tiffany was a thick girl, big-boned and down-to-earth, but at that moment, Rashia only saw red in her vision.

"Don't make me tell you again, Tiffany. Move." Rashia attempted to step around her, and Tiffany reached up to take her by the shoulder.

"Listen to me—"

That was as far as Tiffany got before her head snapped back violently from the vicious uppercut strike Rashia delivered.

Then she followed through with a mean overhand punch that dropped Tiffany like a bad habit. People all around the room were astounded by this action. Then, when Rashia went marching towards the office, several women bolted from their chairs and hurried for the exit door. No one wanted to be present for what they figured Rashia was about to do.

The office door was shut, but you could hear Trina talking on the phone inside. That's all Rashia needed to hear, and she kicked the door in and went inside. Trina, startled by the invasion, jumped up to her feet when Rashia came through the door. Then Rashia rushed her hard and bashed her in the face with the pistol. The blow sent Trina crashing into the wall behind the desk, and that's where Rashia got on her ass something fierce.

It wasn't long before Trina was screaming for help as Rashia gave her a thrashing, but help did come in the form of two stylists and a guy that wasn't in the building just a minute ago. They had to double up on Rashia to pull her off Trina, but that only got them staring down the barrel of her bloody pistol and her demanding them to back the fuck up.

"Put your hands on me again, and I'll shoot you dead in your shit," sneered Rashia, swinging the pistol from one to the other.

Behind her, Trina was whimpering and groaning in excruciating pain and agony. Her face was fucked up, her teeth caved in, and blood was all over the wall and floor. Rashia came to take care of business, and she did just that.

"Now, bitch." Rashia turned back to Trina with that dark look on her face. "I want my money. I want what's owed to me and for wastin' my goddamn time. And it better look right, or else I'ma shoot your stupid ass next."

The two stylists, Dominique and Anna, were working together to help Trina up and giving her false hope that everything would be alright.

"Bitch, write that check up," said Rashia.

She then glared at the guy still present in the room.

"Who the fuck are you?"

"I'm Eboni's people," he said.

"Then go find Eboni and get the hell outta my business."

Eboni was one of the other stylists who worked wonders with nail designs. He shook his head and left.

With the help of the others, Trina located her checkbook and wrote out a check to Rashia as she demanded. When she was handed the check, Rashia only nodded once and stored it in the pocket of her jeans.

"Fuck you, Trina. All you had to do was respect my mind," said Rashia. "Now we're enemies, bitch. And if you wanna test this shit again, you better have your shit together next time."

Then she walked out without another word. There was blood in her eyes. That beast had awakened.

***

Later . . .

Quan moved before the group of killers and some of his closest homeboys and business associates alike. The expression he was carrying was tense but filled with disappointment and contempt. Quan had something to say, and by all means, they all better take heed, or there would be consequences.

"Zion Griffen is off-limits. The hit on his head has been lifted," he said.

"Is he dead already?" asked Rod.

"No," Quan replied. "What I'm saying is that he is not to be touched. Zy is not the enemy. I gave him something with the order to protect it with his life."

"What did you give him?"

"That's neither here nor there, Skip. When them people pulled me over on some bullshit, Zy jeopardized himself to save me," said Quan.

Also standing to the right of him was Yvonnie. She was looking quite disturbed and apparently saddened over what had taken place with her family. Still, her family hadn't turned back up yet. Sheena did not keep her end of the bargain, and Yvonnie felt stupid for even believing that she would. That bitch was heartless, and when it came down to flexin' her murder game, she did her shit in style.

Quan went on to express the loss of their own men to this whole thing.

"Yvonnie was only acting in accordance with what she expected me to do if the shoe was on the other foot."

"So we just let them get away with killin' Rocko and 'em?" asked Tron, one of the younger goons who actually looked up to Rocko and Prep.

"In a situation like this, yes. Because like I was saying, Zy didn't do nothing wrong, and his people was only there to protect their own."

"Sheena," said another.

"Right. Someone who has put in work for this team for years. And as for Oscar, he was defending his brotha. I don't see nothing wrong with that. I woulda done the same for any one of y'all. It all was just a misunderstanding, and I'm asking y'all to stand down on this one." Quan glanced over at Yvonnie and scowled menacingly.

"And if they continue to strike out at us? We just let that shit ride?" asked Favion.

"I'ma reach out to them and try to put an end to this shit, lil' brotha. I got this," Quan said.

"What about Yvonnie's family though? My grandma was her grandma. I'm not lettin' that shit slide," said Lil' Ren.

Again, Quan looked over at Yvonnie.

"C'mere, Ren." Yvonnie called her cousin forward with a wave, and he separated himself from the group to make his way over.

"What're you doing, Yvonnie?" muttered Quan, watching as Lil' Ren approached them.

"The ultimate sacrifice," Yvonnie said and drew her gun. When Lil' Ren came to stand before her, she shot him dead center in his forehead.

This shocked everybody in the room, even Quan, who knew Lil' Ren was adored by his cousin.

"Y'all see this shit?" Yvonnie let her voice be heard over the room. "Yes, I'm to blame for why we're all in here right now. I did what I did because I was personally under the impression that my man had been crossed. And we lost some good niggaz because of that decision. But before I allow that to happen again and have Ren go after them and cause us another war—and possibly more death for our team—I killed him. I murdered my own flesh and blood for the greater good of our team—our family. This is what we signed up for, gentlemen. We live and we learn. Today I've learned a very valuable lesson," she said.

"And was it worth it?" Quan asked.

"Yes."

"What did you learn from all this?"

"Patience," she replied. "Patience and humility. It is necessary that we exercise those two traits to the best of our ability."

"Again," Quan spoke up. "Zion is not to be touched. He's family. I literally watched him grow up in the hood. He's a good kid. So take this situation and use it as a lesson learned."

When the meeting finally ended, Quan sent Yvonnie on her way while he stayed behind to discuss some things with his new chief of enforcers. This was a longtime friend of his by the name of Ced, who was taking the place of Trill.

"What's up, Q? Talk to me," said Ced, whose new position had been granted by the favorable votes from the team's councils.

"I think it's time to get Bo Henderson out the way for good."

"He did that to your face?"

Quan nodded. "I provoked him," he said. "But most importantly, I think Tony is the one that Bo's getting his information from."

"Oh, really." Ced stroked his goatee.

"And I don't think he's up in Memphis neither. I believe he's laying low around here somewhere. I don't like it, Ced. I want both of them gone, understood?"

"Understood."

The two shook hands.

After a few more things were discussed with his chief enforcer, Quan exited the warehouse to find Donte waiting outside for him. He and Donte looked at each other, then Quan finally approached him.

"You okay, brotha?"

"For the most part," shrugged Quan.

"Good. C'mon, let's spin a few blocks so we can have a talk and settle a few thangs."

"This sounds serious."

"It is," said Donte. "I miss my muthafuckin brotha, nigga. I'm just tryna make it right."

Chapter 14

Oscar leaned into the driver side window of the forest green Acura and placed his lips against those of his girlfriend, Joya. She had been blowing his phone up, demanding that he answer. Joya was worried why her man didn't show up at their afternoon date at Dairy Queen. Then on top of that, she had heard the rumors regarding Zion, and that alone deepened her concern.

"I love you," said Oscar. "I got work to do. I'll get up wit' you later when I can."

"You promise?"

He shook his head. "Promises are meant to be broken, so don't take any of them from nobody."

Joya nodded, and he saluted her. Then she waved at Oscar before driving away with her cousin Bre riding next to her. After watching the car turn the corner up the street, Oscar snapped back in beast-mode. The sinister look in his eyes at that moment was for what he was about to do.

"You ready?" Sheena asked him.

"You know I am."

Oscar circled around the car to get in on the passenger side. They had just dropped Tabitha off in High Bridge to be with her boyfriend, Lex, for now. He was ordered to keep her safely inside, behind closed doors, until they heard back from them only. They were going to rescue Zion, but first, some blood had to be spilled.

It was already verified who the two perpetrators were that Lyric had sent after Zion earlier. One of them was Spank from the Circle Drive area, who was also Lyric's cousin — recently released from prison after doing ten years. And the other was Jitt from East Quincy, someone Spank had no past dealings with until they linked up three years ago at some other prison institution.

They did all that time in prison, only to die less than a year and four weeks after getting out. Their current location was also verified through a reliable source of Sheena's. Both Spank and Jitt were over in the New Projectz, hanging out, shooting the breeze. Little did they know this was one of Oscar's favorite spots to be. He grew up in the New Projectz before his moms moved them over across the road into Lake Skillet. It was still pretty much home to Oscar, but it was also home to one of Sheena's proteges — Dawn Simmons.

It was Dawn who had them two niggaz currently in her scope. She wanted to go ahead and press play on them, but Sheena explained to her the personal relevance of the matter. That's when Sheena's phone rang, and she checked the display to see who it was. When she saw Donte's number, she hesitated before taking his call.

"Make it fast," she said. "I'm busy."

"A truce is all I want, Sheena."

She frowned at the sound of Quan's voice.

"It's because of you this shit is even happening."

"Who's that, Sheena?" Oscar asked.

Quan told her what happened and what was also done about it on his end.

"I've ordered my people to stand down," he claimed.

"You know I've always valued your word, right, Quan?" she replied.

"That's what I'm asking you to do now. I'm sorry, Sheena. I never meant for any of this shit to happen. I take full responsibility."

"So you're owning up to the matter?"

"I am."

Sheena chewed on her bottom lip as Oscar stared unblinkingly at her.

"It's gold as always. But when this mess is all said and done, Quan, I want you to shoot me that fade. Or else. Put Yvonnie in there. It doesn't matter."

"I'ma honor that, baby."

They spoke further on the matter, with Donte voicing his concerns as well. Then Sheena ended their communication when they finally reached their destination of the New Projectz. It was as if Dawn had a tracking device on them, because just as soon as Sheena turned into the first entrance from Two o'clock BP Station way, her text message came through.

"Change of plans," she read. "They're headin' out right now. Subjectz on the move."

"In what?" was Sheena's reply.

"A white Cadillac Escalade wit' Junior."

"Shit." Sheena cussed when she saw the big truck coming near them up ahead.

She was in an unmarked vehicle, so Spank and Jitt were clueless as to what they were ridin' in.

"I'll handle it," said Oscar.

"You sure? Okay. Spare Junior, though. I don't want him to get hurt, Oscar," she pleaded with him, knowing how destructive he could get at times.

The SUV was riding over the last speed bump before the short straightaway shot to the mouth of the entrance key. Just when it looked like Sheena were about to drive past, she yoked the wheel hard as the car suddenly turned into its path. The truck braked hard. By this time, Oscar was already out the car, toting his Draco assault rifle and sending rounds through the windshield.

Through quick observation, it was confirmed that Junior was the driver. So Oscar aimed his monster to the passenger side of the truck. He literally sprayed the paint off that bitch as automatic rounds ripped through the right side of the truck. From the front passenger side to the back, Oscar didn't let up on the trigger till forty-three rounds had been shot.

Junior had taken the risk to jump out the truck and get away, leaving its occupants to their deaths. Spank had attempted to do the same thing until them hot slugs tore his back up. Of course, Oscar made sure of that. It's very rare that he misses.

***

With a deep breath, Zion stepped around the corner and ran smacked right into Rashia. The vase of flowers she had in her hand was in the process of flying out her hand until his quick reflexes recovered the vase before it hit the floor. Otherwise, it would have been a disaster, and Zion's cover would have been blown.

"I'm sorry," he handed her back the vase.

"That's my bad too," said Rashia, accepting the vase and inspecting the flowers within. "I wasn't paying attention."

"No, *I* wasn't paying attention."

Rashia looked at him skeptically. "Don't I know you, youngin'?" she asked.

He shrugged. Zion was wearing a designer face mask that Coach Thomas had given him, so he didn't know how she was able to recognize him enough to know who he was behind the mask.

"I gotta go," he said quickly and stepped around her, heading down the hallway.

He was occupying the ICU ward, searching for the correct number above the room door he was looking for. He then found the room and slipped inside.

There were two people occupying the room. One of them being Sheila Mae Brown, and she was the older woman lying in the bed asleep. The other was a much younger female that Zion recognized but didn't know personally.

"Zion," said the one sitting next to the bed by the window.

She had been in the process of reading some novel but set it aside when Zion entered the room. Zion still had the mask covering majority of his face. Her recognizing him too was astonishing, so he removed the mask and pocketed it.

"You would try to disguise yourself when you got the whole world watching for you."

"No, I don't."

"The Town's Golden Child. Now you've gone and earned yourself the wrong attention behind that mess wit' my uncle Quan. It's all over social media. I've read and heard all about it."

"You shouldn't believe everything you hear."

"I don't, Zion."

He moved forward to come stand at the foot of the bed. The woman lying in it was sweet as rice pudding, always had a kind word to say. A virtuous woman of integrity that Zion knew without a doubt didn't deserve this fate. Her heart was pure.

Zion remembered his mother talking about Quan's sick mother. He had been so busy in school and focusing on his own self-growth that he didn't think about the sweet older lady who always made him grin. Sheila Mae was a charming woman, and then he remembered her. Right when his thoughts of survival had taken control. He knew of all places to look for him and be prevented from harm was right here. He was safe right here.

"What's your name?" he asked.

"Heather."

Then it finally hit him like a fullback on the twenty-yard line. Heather. Heather Banks, the girl with the limp, the one who left home after high school and went into the Navy.

"Remember me now?" Heather asked him, seeing the connection pass through him.

"You used to babysit me when I was little," he said awkwardly.

"Well," Heather smiled sadly, "you ain't so little no more, golden child."

Chapter 15

Nineteen minutes later, Heather was staring down into her lap in deep thought. Zion had just admitted to everything he'd gone through since leaving Quan behind to fend for himself. Although she had learned what she could through social media, hearing Zion tell his side was nightmarish in a sense. He had literally been marked for death.

Heather said, "It's a wonder why God blessed you with speed the way he did."

He only just shifted in his seat.

"You ran for your life, Zion, and now you still have your life to keep," she added.

"How'd you figure that?"

"Because," Heather said, just before the monitor next to the bed began its alarming whine.

She jerked her head toward the bed and saw that Quan's mother was flatlining.

"No," Zion panicked.

Heather then dived for the emergency button by the bed and punched it. Instantly, the Code Red signal was raised, and moments afterward the door opened as a team of medical personnel rushed inside.

Both Heather and Zion were standing aside watching as they worked to save Sheila. Then they both were ordered to leave the room, but Heather wasn't having it; she was panicking like crazy.

"C'mon, Heather." Zion wrapped his arm around her, and that's when she broke down.

The flatline sound from the monitor sounded like a hideous version of a stuck piano key pressed down.

Out in the hallway outside the door, Zion held Heather in his arms and whispered words of comfort, and then Yvonnie turned the corner onto the walkway of the hallway, moving in their direction. When she recognized Zion, she halted, observed the scene for a second, then took off running in their direction.

Zion glanced up at her and stepped away, drawing the Beretta and aiming it at her.

"Stop!" he ordered her.

Yvonnie stopped four feet from the door. Then she looked at Heather and said, "Niecey, what's the matter with you?"

"It's Nana," cried Heather miserably.

"What happened?"

"She flatlined," Heather told her, and Yvonnie went in panic mode.

Yvonnie looked at Zion and told him he would just have to shoot her, because she was going inside the room, and that's what she did exactly — brushed past them and entered the room. Moments later, Yvonnie let out a sorrowful cry that sent Heather rushing back into the room.

Left out in the hallway by himself with a chrome Beretta in his hand, Zion looked around him and saw multiple pairs of eyes staring at him.

"Drop the gun!" a voice demanded.

When Zion looked behind him, he saw two plainclothes detectives drawing down on him. One of them was Detective Bo Henderson, who was now clutching his standard Glock 9mm and sporting a black eye.

"Put the gun down, son. Just drop it," Bo said, gripping his gun with both hands now, sighting down its barrel at Zion.

Right then, the door to Sheila's room opened and Yvonnie stormed out into the hallway. That's when Zion took off running up the hallway in the opposite direction.

"Stop running!"

That was all Zion heard before he bent a quick right around the corner like he was running an option play. It was on to the foot race after that. You wasn't catching him at all. Zion was too fast.

***

Donte had just dropped Quan off out in the country of St. John to retrieve his car when he got the call about his mother. It was there, behind the wheel of his Ford Mustang, that he sobbed like a baby — alone and fighting the urge to do something drastic.

After about ten minutes of letting himself go in his grief, Quan started up the car and headed out to the hospital. He was distraught and broken inside. The very same day he was supposed to finance his mother's operation . . . she dies on him. Quan felt so guilty over it. His worst nightmare had become his reality — his pain and suffering.

Quan cried all the way to the hospital. When he finally reached his destination, there were about ten of his men outside waiting to receive him. He got out the car, which he parked just outside the entrance door of the ER. The group of men parted to allow him to enter the building.

"Them crackaz locked down the place," said Ced, walking alongside his superior, "but we already informed them of your situation."

"Where is she?"

"They took her out to the morgue, awaiting supervision and next of kin to identify her."

"I'm talkin' about Heather," he said.

"Oh," Ced replied.

It was a brief moment before he continued.

"She's searching for Zion."

"Zion?" Quan paused.

"Yeah. That's why Bo and his people locked down the place."

"So Zy's inside the hospital?"

"Apparently."

To hear that Detective Bo was in the building soured Quan's mood even more. He just hoped that Bo never got in his way right now. There was no telling how his inner beast would go once it had been provoked.

"Find Heather and bring her to me," Quan said as he rubbed his weary eyes.

"What about Yvonnie?" he asked.

"What about her?"

Ced stroked his goatee and summoned a couple of his men to go retrieve Heather. Then he and Quan bypassed a team of policemen and hospital security for the morgue. Quan wanted to see his mother one last time before he snapped and never saw her again at all.

At the morgue's door, Quan paused for a long moment, willing himself to remain strong in order to get through this phase.

"I'll accompany you if you want?" said a feminine voice to Quan's left.

When he looked, there stood his sister Melodi, and Quan felt his shattered heart move at the sight of her. It was the pain in her eyes that moved him so — a pain that was similar to his.

"I'll let y'all do what you do while I go check on thangz around the way," said Ced, looking between the two, and walked away.

"Ced?"

Ced glanced over his shoulder.

Quan said, "Thank you, my nigga."

Ced nodded solemnly and continued on his way as Melodi stepped toward Quan and took him carefully by the hand and placed a kiss upon his cheek.

"We gon' go through this together," she said.

He nodded with a deep sigh, and then the door was opened. They went inside, not knowing the hell that very moment was going to cause them both.

Inside, the assigned mortician was just covering the head of Quan's mother when they suddenly walked through the door. Upon entrance, Melodi noticed the saddened look in the mortician's eyes before he gazed up and saw them standing in the lobby. He was a middle-aged white guy in a lab coat, and surprisingly, dark gray hair covered his head. At the sight of them, the man stuffed his hands into the pockets of the lab coat and made his way over to meet them in the lobby.

"Quan da sun," said the mortician.

"Hey, Joe," Quan answered, obviously aware who the man was standing in front of him.

"I'm sorry about what happened. Your mother was a great woman," he replied. "In the thirty or so years she'd worked here in this building with me, Sheila had been the light of our world. Such a sweet creature, she was."

"She's not suffering no more," Quan said.

"Not at all."

"I just wanna talk to me girl, Joe. Just one last time," Quan grieved, and the mortician was more than accepting about it.

Joe showed him where his mother was and peeled back the sheet covering her face. Then he left them be to share their moment.

"He loved her," said Melodi.

"Who didn't?" Quan whimpered unashamed. "Everybody loved my baby."

Everybody did. Sheila Mae Brown was an incredible woman.

Chapter 16

Zion was exactly where he wanted to be, which was standing there at Candice's bedside. He was fighting the hardest battle ever to keep from crying over the girl he loved. The same girl whose life was hanging on by a thread because of him.

If only Kelli hadn't seen him leaving them, maybe Candice wouldn't be here, and they all would still be alive — except for him, maybe. Because his exposure at that time probably would have been the cause of his early death if them niggas would have seen him. Because there's only so many times he could run and get away.

As for his current position, Coach Thomas played a part in him duping the officials. He and Melodi. If they didn't believe in him as a good person, or the true love he had for Candice, then Zion might just have been shit out of luck.

The golden child.

That goldenness was surely working its magic in his continuous survival.

Zion gazed down upon Candice, and his heart did some things to him. He really loved this girl. Loved her since the moment he laid eyes on her all those years ago.

"I'm sorry," he said for the hundredth time, hoping somewhere deep down in her consciousness state of existence that she could hear his cries.

It had been two close calls when Candice flatlined in result of her injuries. She had been shot in the neck and in the chest, and yet here she was, still breathing. Barely breathing on her own, because now she was on life support, connected to a respirator.

The girl had more tubes protruding from her body than a goddamn laptop computer, but she was fighting. Candice had always been a tough little cookie. She was a fighter. Refused to be defeated by anything under the sun, which is one of the reasons why Zion loved her.

Candice was competitive. She was stubborn.

"And I'll never take you for granted again," Zion replied through his emotions.

"You better not," came Quan's voice as he entered the room with Melodi in tow.

At the sight of him, Zion frowned and walked up to Quan and punched him so hard in the face. Melodi braced herself for a battle.

"I'll take that," said Quan, rubbing his throbbing jaw and testing it to make sure Zion hadn't broken it with his vicious left hook. "I deserve all that, lil' Zy."

Zion was tempted to swing on him more, but instead he turned back toward Candice and reclaimed his spot at her bedside.

Every time Melodi looked at Zion and saw the love in his eyes that he had for her daughter, she just wanted to wrap him in her arms. She believed if there ever was a chance of Zion going professional and wanting to start his own family legacy, it would be with Candice. It was so amazing to see a young love like this so strong and unwavering.

Then there was De'Kari, thought Melodi, with dismay etched on her face. She didn't see what Candice saw in his friend Jamir. The boy was literally De'Kari's puppet. It was De'Kari who was influencing how Jamir should treat her daughter. It was as if De'Kari himself wanted Candice but was letting Jamir have her through his own personal desires.

Where they do that at?

Melodi wished that Zion would finally man up and claim Candice as his own and stop bullshitting.

"If I'd known you would have gone through all that shit, lil' Zy, I wouldn't have told you to do that," said Quan.

Zion looked at him darkly.

"My mama was kidnapped. My cousin was killed. And CANDICE!" He was breathing fire at that moment, and Melodi had to move over to place a hand gently upon his right shoulder. "I was shot in my back . . . if it wasn't for the money stopping the bullet."

Then he went into further detail about what he had to go through trying to secure the money. Zion had tears of rage and anguish spilling from his eyes.

Quan felt like shit.

That's when Zion unstrapped the backpack from behind him and threw it at Quan's feet. Quan looked down at the bag quietly, then picked it up to look inside.

"I only took one of the stacks."

"The one that stopped the bullet?" Melodi had said in understanding of where Zion was going in the statement he just made.

For a moment, Quan stood there with the bag in his hands, with an indecisive look on his face. Then he walked up to Zion and shoved the bag into his arms.

"Here," he said. "This is all yours to have. I don't need it no more anyway. You need it more than I do."

Zion just stared down at the money.

"I know it's nothing compared to the damage that was done," continued Quan. "But it's a start."

"What was it for in the first place?" asked Zion.

"My mama."

Zion looked at him awkwardly. "Mz. Sheila?"

It was at that moment that Quan explained to him the real reason that money existed.

When Zion heard this, his heart squeezed with anguish. Then Quan began to cry. This was a shock to both Melodi and Zion. To see Quan cry. It was like watching the Grim Reaper cry.

Then suddenly, the door opened, and the very last person they expected to see stepped inside.

Detective Bo.

And that's when things got hectic.

***

It was minutes away before the streetlights came when Peggie Bradwell turned onto the path leading to Tabitha's front door. This was Oscar's mother, the town's trick and one of the biggest cokeheads in the area. Oscar had long ago stopped being ashamed of his mother — her life was her life, and he couldn't live it for her. The only thing he could do was keep on pushing and striving to make the best out of his own life.

Peggie had heard the latest news about what took place with Zion. Then the situation regarding her own son and his loyalty to Zion. It didn't surprise her to hear how Oscar had put it down earlier. She'd grown accustomed to seeing his street reputation flourish. Her son was a force to be reckoned with. He was thuggin', but she still was a concerned mother, and that's why she was there now.

As Peggie made her way to the front door of the house, Matilda was pulling up in her driveway next door. Peggie continued her mission and knocked on the front door and waited.

"How ya doing, Peg?" greeted Matilda, stepping before the back door of her car to grab the few bags of groceries she had on the back seat.

Peggie glanced her way and waved briefly, then she turned for the door again and knocked. Harder this time, and then the door caved inwardly a little bit. Instantly, Peggie took a step back and examined the door, coming to terms with what may have happened here.

"Oh damn," she muttered.

A horn honked behind her, and when she looked back, there was Oscar. He swung the car over to the curb and jumped out at once.

"Mama, what are you doing?" he said, walking across the front lawn toward her.

"I was lookin' for you," she said.

"You can't be out here like this, ma. It's dangerous. It's war in these streets right now," Oscar replied in a rush of words.

A pair of headlights turned onto the street up ahead, and Oscar caught the move. Out the passenger window protruded a hooded gunman with what looked like an assault rifle. Instantly, Oscar drew his pistol when the first shot rang out.

"Mama!" Oscar cried out as his Glock .40 blasted off shots at the car as he dashed across the grass toward his mother.

The drive-by shooter didn't let up as she shattered the silence of the evening with automatic rounds, but Oscar wasn't slacking up either as he blasted on them fools. Two feet from his mother, Oscar felt three slugs punch him in the back, pitching him forward in collision with Peggie. They fell to the ground hard, with Oscar landing on top of his mother, holding her down protectively.

"Ohmigod! Baby!" Peggie cried.

"My vest, Ma," Oscar groaned in tremendous pain as he weighed his mother down with his body. "My vest took the bullets," he told her.

But Peggie was not convinced of this when she felt the warm sensation of something spreading under him.

"Get up, baby. You squashing me!"

Oscar bellowed in agony as he rolled off the top of her, and that's when he saw what it was — blood all over her clothes. Then she looked at Oscar and saw him bleeding profusely from his left leg.

"You've been hit, baby. Oh Lord! They done shot my baby!" she panicked.

Sure enough, one of the bullets found its way into the back of Oscar's left thigh. Oscar growled in pain and discomfort as he lay on his side trying not to move.

Out of nowhere, Jabo rushed to the scene, and with the help of Peggie and Matilda, they managed to get Oscar into the car and driven away into the night.

With Jabo behind the wheel, Oscar roared like a wounded lion, telling his mother to remove the vest he had on. Despite his crucial predicament, Oscar was still focused enough to remain on point, because just as soon as them people found that bulletproof vest on him, there would be hell to pay. So Peggie disposed of the vest by stuffing it underneath the passenger seat.

At the hospital, Oscar was taken into immediate surgery and raising hell along the way. Standing outside the operating room, Peggie looked up and saw Rashia headed her way.

This was someone whom Peggie hadn't seen in weeks — the daughter of her good friend Carla, who passed away years ago when Rashia was young. Although Peggie had her own thing going on, she still found time for Rashia whenever they bumped into each other.

Rashia said, "I thought that was you I saw come through here."

"Oscar was shot tonight."

This astounded Rashia, very aware how Peggie's son got it in out there in the trenches. Then she looked at Peggie and saw her dress in blood, knowing the woman was going through a very rough time at the risk of losing her child.

"Where was he shot?"

"In the leg," Peggie replied.

"Then you need to be grateful for that, because the way thangs going out there right now, it could've been worse."

That was a truth Peggie knew without a doubt. Because if her son wouldn't have been wearing that vest, she would have been devastated. Oscar would be dead.

So yeah. She had plenty reasons to be grateful. She just hoped Oscar would see the blessing in that situation like it was meant for him to see. That he could be touched too. That he wasn't invincible. He wasn't God.

Chapter 17

Almost out of the recently developed habit he'd been forced to take, Zion instinctively reached for his waistline for a gun that wasn't there. Because of his critical predicament, Coach Thomas took it upon himself to dispose of the gun. Though Quan would have liked to have his Beretta back for just this purpose.

Detective Bo Henderson thought shit was sweet.

The man was crazy.

"I see we meet again," snarled Bo.

"This nigga must got a death wish or something," said Quan.

"You know," Bo tugged on his right earlobe thoughtfully for a second. "I always wondered that but convinced myself I don't have a death wish, because I'm still alive," he chuckled.

"What do you want, Bo?" Melodi replied. "Can't you see we are grieving right now?"

"Why grieve when there's still life, Melodi?" Bo gestured towards the bed. "I came to ask you a few questions regarding your daughter's situation, only to find out you've been hoarding a fugitive this whole time," he said.

"A fugitive? Who?"

The detective's gaze landed on Zion, but just when he opened his mouth to speak, the door behind him opened. It was Moby who entered the room, and this seemed to displease Bo.

"What are you doing, Bo?" Moby demanded.

"Just a few questions for the lady, Moby. No problems whatsoever. Didn't know these were your people," Bo's voice sounded funny.

"Well, this ain't the time for that. Go find you somebody else to worry," said Moby.

"No problem," Bo said.

For a long moment, no one moved. Then Moby stepped aside and gestured toward the door that he wanted Bo to leave out of. With another lasting glance in Zion's direction, the detective moved for the door and found his way out. Moby was tempted to slap him in the back of the head in passing.

When the door shut closed behind the detective, it was then that Zion turned his gaze on him quizzically. Or was it confusion?

"What the hell was that about?" asked Melodi, beating the others to the punch.

"That's a first," said Quan with surprise. "What do you got on that creep?"

"What makes you think I got something on him, Quan?"

"The man was literally shaking in his boots when you popped up just now. In all the years I've known that nigga, I never seen that. You got something on him. I don't give a fuck how you try to shake the truth. You got him shook."

"He's a pedophile," said Moby.

"Huh?"

"Been blackmailing that nigga for the past six years, when I caught him fucking around with little kids. Remember that little boy over in Havana that went missing from summer camp all those years ago? They assumed that a gator had snatched him up and dragged him into the lake?"

"Bo was the gator," said Quan with a shake of his head.

"That's so sick," Melodi said sourly.

"But you can kill him now if you want to, Quan. I have no use for him anymore. I was gonna do it, but seeing what he did to you, I think you'll find satisfaction in sending him to his grave."

Moby didn't care about speaking so freely around them, because he knew it would never be used against him.

Zion reflected back on that last look Bo gave him, and it made him queasy. He wanted someone to off him now. Bo should have been dead.

"As I said earlier, the nigga got a death wish," said Quan.

"That he surely does." Moby then moved toward Melodi and gathered her into his arms and placed a gentle kiss upon her cheek. "I came back like I promised," he told her.

"But you didn't bring it though."

"I did."

"Where are they then?"

That's when he dug into the pocket of his pants and extracted a pack of Newports. When Melodi reached for the cigarettes, he moved them out of her reach.

"Moby!" she frowned.

"You haven't smoked in ten years, Melodi, and this ain't no reason for you to start back now," he said.

"Then why did you bring it?"

"Because," Moby replied with a smirk on his rugged face, "I just wanted to show you that I'm still willing to do anything for your ass. Just nothing that's bad for you, Melodi."

Both Quan and Zion looked at one another awkwardly and decided it was time that they leave to give them space.

"I'll be back for Candice, Mz. Mel," said Zion, seeing what's going on.

"But you don't have to leave," she said.

"I do," he answered. "I still have obligations to fulfill. I'll come back later. Trust that. I am gonna come back to her."

"I know," Melodi replied, resting her head onto Moby's shoulder. "I know you are."

Then Zion and Quan took their leave, only to walk into something so disturbing that it made Zion's heart hurt.

Then the inner beast was released.

***

"It was Loony that did it," said Jabo, standing outside the hospital face to face with Zion nineteen minutes later.

At the mention of Loony being responsible for what happened to his friend, Zion became consumed by rage at its highest level. Also present was Lyshelle Cooper, the other close friend of Candice who graduated a year prior and was currently attending FAMU. They all were from the same neighborhood.

"A'ight," Zion replied. "Let's go!"

"No, Zee." Lyshelle grabbed him by the arm.

Zion roughly snatched away from her.

"That muthafucker shot my brotha," he scowled.

"So now you're gonna go shoot him back?"

"If that's what it takes." Zion turned away from her, and this time she restrained him with both hands to stop him. Just like he does on the field when breaking a tackle, Zion shook her off and mistakenly hit her with an elbow that sent her flailing off balance.

"I gotcha," Lyshelle heard someone say after sensing them catch her fall before she hit the ground.

When she looked up, she was surprised to see a total stranger there — but not just any total stranger. It was Rashia that stepped up just in time.

"Thank you, ma'am."

"What's going on? Everything alright?"

"My stupid homeboy about to go do something stupid that'll prolly get himself killed. It's bad enough that Oscar almost got done in tonight already."

"I saw Oscar earlier . . . is he okay?" Rashia asked.

After realizing she said way too much, Lyshelle excused herself and rushed back into the hospital. There was no secret where she was going next.

Meanwhile, Rashia looked up at the retreat of Zion and Jabo, who hurriedly jumped into a nearby car and proceeded to drive off. Quickly, Rashia hurried over to her own vehicle and got in to go follow them and see what's what.

Up ahead, Zion was sitting in the front seat of the car that Jabo was in the process of driving. He had been so caught up in the moment that he didn't stop to realize that he was in the company of someone less likely to have his back when the pressure is applied.

"Jabo, who car this is?" Zion smelled the potent scent of blood inside and turned around in his seat.

"Oscar's," he said.

"This is not my brotha's car."

"It's what he was driving before that shit went down," said Jabo.

Then he re-elaborated on what took place at the house before he and Peggie rushed Oscar to the hospital. When he mentioned the bulletproof vest, Zion reached beneath the passenger seat in search of it. He felt something, but it wouldn't budge until he grabbed it with two hands and pulled it from beneath him.

"Oh yeah," Jabo replied, materializing with a gun that he said belonged to Oscar. "It's what he was using when they shot him."

In what little light he could use, Zion situated the bulletproof vest after locating the three projectiles indenting the back of the vest. Figuring it would still be in good use, Zion managed to put on the vest and secured it. Then he took possession of the gun Jabo said belonged to his brother and clutched it tightly.

"So we're going back to the hood?"

Zion thought about it for a moment, believing that it was Jamir who sent the hit through his big brother because of what he did to him earlier. Zion had no clue that it was Oscar that actually sparked the fuse. When he shot up De'Kari's house, that prompted Loony to respond back in the same fashion.

That evening, it was De'Kari that got grazed across the face by one of the bullets. That's all Loony needed to see to know how easily that could have been Jamir.

"I want Loony for what he did."

"Not Jamir or the others?"

Zion shook his head. "No. Loony is the threat, and he's too dangerous to let live."

"Okay," said Jabo. "Let's find Loony then."

Chapter 18

When Tabitha heard the news about Oscar being shot, she disregarded her orders given by Sheena and her son, and made Lex take her to the hospital.

By the time she made it there, she was surprised to see that Oscar's girlfriend, Joya, had just arrived as well. Together they went inside the hospital and were directed to Oscar's room.

Upon entering the room, Oscar was in the process of raising hell. He wanted out, but his mother was being quite stubborn about it.

"Good. Y'all deal wit' his ass," said Peggie when they walked through the door.

Joya rushed to his side at once, but Oscar didn't want no affection or to be pitied; he wanted to get back to the streets.

"He was good till that girl came in here going on about your boy," Peggie said, looking at Tabitha.

"Zion? What about my son?"

Peggie removed herself from her son's bedside to come stand in front of the other woman.

"Zee has gone after the boy that shot Oscar. And that's what's driving this one crazy — he's worried about his brotha," she explained.

Before Tabitha could allow herself to panic, the door opened and Quan entered. He had a cellphone to his ear and looked at Tabitha with open surprise.

"I got Tab right here, my nigga."

"Who is that?" she asked Quan.

He offered her the phone, and she put it to her ear.

"Who is this?"

"This me, cuz. Spud. What's going on wit' my little nigga out there?"

This was Spud Conyers, the son of Tabitha's uncle Andrew, and the very same nigga who was Tabitha's hero when he was home. At the sound of her cousin's voice, Tabitha exploded with her concerns on everything.

Meanwhile, Quan slid over to where Oscar and Joya was and was going back and forth with Oscar about Zion's situation.

"You know we can't lose him, cuz," said Spud, having contacted Quan by one of the many cellphones that was smuggled into the prison he was at. "Because all it takes is one kill and he'll never be the same."

"I know," Tabitha sighed. "I'ma get Quan on it as soon as possible," she said.

"Where's Sheena at?"

"She's around. She took a loss today, too."

"Who?"

"Lyric."

"Damn," muttered Spud.

Tabitha then spoke in code that it was Zion who had killed Lyric, and why.

"That's why I think it's already too late for him, Spud."

Spud didn't say anything for a long time.

"I love you, cuz. Lemme talk to Quan. Don't worry, we gon' do what we can to save him. Just don't go out there tryna be no fuckin' hero."

"But he's my son, Spud," she whined.

When Lex witnessed this, he rushed over to her side.

"Just do what the fuck I say, cuz. Stay safe and pray like you always do. Now put Quan on the phone, because I'm losing my damn patience."

With a long sigh, she called Quan to the phone.

"You stay put," Quan told her, already knowing where her head was.

Oscar said, "C'mere, Mama Tee." He beckoned her over while Joya clutched to his right hand.

He was hurting — you could see it in his eyes — but Oscar was too headstrong to admit it. Tabitha went to him with pain and fear for her son glazed in her eyes.

"The only thang you can do for my brotha right now is pray," Oscar took her by the hand.

"Spud just said the same thing."

"He's smart. Zion, I mean. And he's the fastest person I know. Wit' those two gifts combined, he cannot be touched," said Oscar. "The nigga won't let nothin' happen to him 'cause he know it'll kill you."

"Or I kill the person that hurts my baby."

"He's good, Mama Tee."

"No, he's not," said Tabitha. "Zion is running scared out there and doesn't have a clue what's lurking out there in the shadows waitin' for him."

***

It was Sheena, Dawn, and TJ standing in the middle of the Black Top basketball court out in Pepper Hill that evening. Laying on the ground in the middle of their formed circle was Yvonnie.

She had called herself cornering Sheena when she spotted her at the 24-hour Kelly Jr. getting gas. By the time she even got up on Sheena, her two protégés already had her cornered and restrained.

Right then, Sheena was supposed to kill her ass, but was patient in her response. Instead, her two goons forced Yvonnie into the backseat of the SUV they rode up in and wedged her between them while Sheena took them to a different location.

Not wanting to spend much time with the matter, Yvonnie was taken to the Black Top park over in the Jackson Heights area of Pepper Hill and beaten severely for her actions.

Then Sheena phoned Quan. She wanted to just kill the bitch and be done with it, but because of the respect she had for Quan, she didn't. This was a matter where he had to make a decision.

But then a motorcade of four vehicles pulled up on the scene and parked at the curb. There were three SUVs and a dark sedan, and a total of fourteen people got out.

Instantly, TJ swung his Mac-11 assault rifle in the direction of the group. Dawn kept her gun on Yvonnie while drawing her second weapon and pointing it over at the group.

"Donte," Sheena whispered when the kingpin himself stepped forward where his identity was clear enough.

Still, Sheena didn't budge when Donte made his approach along with three of his men.

"Always hard at work," chuckled Donte when he finally reached the basketball court.

"This wasn't hard work at all, Donte. What do you want? I'm busy here," said Sheena.

"For starters, have your people stand down and drop their guns," he replied.

"I can't do that, Donte."

"I mean aiming them at me and my men. I'm not the enemy, and neither are my men. I only came here for one thang and one thang only."

"Yvonnie?" she said.

He shook his head no. "Makayla," he said. "Where is the girl, Sheena?"

"The girl?" Sheena looked at him sideways.

That was one of the main reasons why Yvonnie called herself cornering her earlier. She had yet to receive her loved ones back, and their absence was weighing on her conscience to the point of insanity.

"I couldn't care less about the others, but that little girl is important. Where is she?"

"Is she yours, Donte?"

"No. She's the daughter of Shane. Now we know you're against killin' kids, but seeing Makayla as she is woulda prevented you from even thinkin' about harming her. So tell me where she is so I can straighten all this mess out wit' Shane. Shit like this makes niggas' time hard, and I'm pretty sure you can relate to that," said Donte, with a hint of knowing her own hardships.

Of course she could relate to that matter.

When Douvie got killed, Sheena was in prison serving her last twenty-four months on a five-year bid. The situation hit her so hard she started cutting up in there and earned herself an additional two years for violent offenses. Sheena took her little cousin's death hard, especially after having just spoken with him an hour before it happened.

That's why she went hard for Zion — because she didn't want him subjected to that same fate.

"What's it gonna be, Sheena? Tell me where she is so you can get back to what you're doing."

"Or what?" she stated curiously.

Donte frowned. "You don't really wanna hurt Shane, so miss me wit' the bullshit."

Blocka!

The gunshot blast startled them all as everybody instantly reacted to the eruption.

"Don't move again," Dawn warned Yvonnie, whose head the bullet missed by a few inches, but the impact of the bullet smashing concrete was enough to inflict pain along the side of her already banged-up face.

"Sheena." Donte was growing impatient.

"She's safe, Donte."

"Where?"

"Where do you want her to be, Donte? She's just a phone call away." Sheena held up her phone, to which she had been about to connect with Quan regarding his bitch.

Donte told her where he wanted little Makayla delivered, and she assured him that she would see that it gets done.

"Okay," he saluted her. "And Yvonnie?"

Yvonnie gazed up at him helplessly.

"You've picked your poison, and I can't save you this time."

Donte turned and walked away, and Yvonnie called out to him to no avail.

Sheena called Quan's number.

He answered. "I already know. I told her to fall back, and she went against my call. Do what you do, Sheena."

The line was disconnected before Sheena even got the first word out.

"Okay. Damn," she replied.

"What did he say?" Dawn asked, both guns still trained on Yvonnie.

"Kill the bitch," she said.

"My pleasure."

Chapter 19

They had driven all through Lake Skillet in search of Loony and didn't find him. Then they headed out to *Friendship* where Loony's right-hand man, Jarvis, lived. It was known that Loony could be found out in *Friendship* or up the block if he wasn't already in the hood.

Sure enough, that's where they found him — posted up on the corner with four other niggas. They were all smoking and hanging out and serving the block as customers came and went.

Although it was too dark inside the car to see who was inside, Zion didn't trust the streetlight beaming down upon those standing beneath it, because in passing, there's a chance that same streetlight could identify the car's occupants.

"I'm just gone slide down until we spin back around, and I'll be on their side of the street," said Zion as he did just that.

Jabo didn't respond. They drove past, with Jabo braking for a second before continuing forward.

Behind them, Rashia swung her car into the driveway of a neighbor's house. She was growing wary just following them around until now. Rashia knew exactly who Loony was; he was the mulatto nigga with the gold teeth, tall and slender-built with dreads — which was who she saw from the short distance, standing amongst the group beneath the streetlight.

Rashia wasn't new to this shit; she was true to this. Seeing the car up ahead drive past their target, she knew there was a high chance they were going to double back on them.

From up the street, Loony turned toward the car moving down the road. He drew his gun and played it off cool like there wasn't no threat in what he may have felt like the car beheld.

"Change of plans," said Zion, popping back up in his seat.

"What? I thought we was about to pull a drive-by on them fools." Jabo sounded disappointed that Zion was changing up the plan. "You scared now?"

"No," Zion said. "I'm far from scared."

"Then what's the problem?"

That's when Zion told him how he wanted to do this. Something came over Zion, and he sensed them doubling back would pose a problem. He wanted to really catch them off guard.

"Okay." Jabo was down for the action.

"Find somewhere to park."

The car was parked around the corner alongside the road. Then they got out and began to walk back the way from which they came. But now they were equipped with heavier artillery than the gun Jabo had taken from Oscar.

On their way to wreak havoc upon Loony for what he did, Zion had switched on the car's dome light to look behind him. That's when he spotted the Draco machine gun on the floor behind the driver seat. It was covered in blood from where Oscar had been bleeding all over the place. Zion didn't care one bit about that, just as long as it got the job done.

But at that moment, it was Jabo who was toting the Draco, tucking it safely against his right leg as he walked. After trying so hard to blend in and get accepted by his street peers, Jabo had developed the mannerisms of those with whom he sought acceptance. No one gave him a chance because of who he was, assuming he wasn't fit for the role of thuggin'.

Whether you believe it or not, Jabo came from a good family of four — both parents and a little six-year-old sister named Porsha. He was one of those sheltered kids who watched all the action out in the streets from his bedroom window. Until he got up in age, now where he wanted to be part of that action so bad, he was willing to do anything. Like now.

Although he knew Zion wasn't living that gangster lifestyle like the others, he wanted to make him proud for believing in him. Jabari Jones was down for whatever. Tonight would prove that fact.

Together they walked side by side. From about twenty yards away, Zion nudged him as they veered off across the front lawn of a neighbor's house. They then cut between two houses and took the route behind the row of houses leading up to the street corner up the road.

Zion's only concern was perhaps walking upon a dog and it sounding off the alarm that would alert the others.

"We almost there," said Zion.

Jabo didn't respond. He was too amped up.

Coming upon the last house on the corner, Zion told Jabo it was crunch time.

Still Jabo did not say one word — he only nodded in response.

"Let's go," said Zion, his adrenaline surging through him like warm water.

Zion finally drew his pistol and crept along the side of the house that would put them directly behind their target. Once they made it to the front of the house, Zion gave the signal and took off in a dash across the front lawn.

During the same time, a car was driving past, and from its two passenger windows burst flame from two semi-automatic weapons. Zion skidded in the grass at the unexpected turn of events.

To his horror, Loony and his whole crew got gunned down right in front of him.

What do you know — although he had been hit, Loony managed to escape, running in their direction. That's when Jabo upped the Draco and shot Loony down with the quickness.

Feeling like he should at least do something, Zion walked up to Loony's fallen form and aimed his gun down at him.

"This is for my brotha," said Zion.

A car pulled up just when he was about to pull the trigger.

"Zion, no! Don't do it! Get in the car," said Rashia.

Zion looked up at her voice.

"Get in the car," she repeated. "Please?"

"C'mon!" Jabo shoved him toward the car at the curb, stepping around dead bodies, and climbed into the car with her.

"You again." Zion placed himself next to her, and then they were gone.

The stench of gunpowder and blood clung to the air — thick, hot, and heavy.

Smoke lingered. Metal, blood, and silence — death had a scent, and it was everywhere.

The air smelled like bodies. Like death just clocked in. Vengeance was served, but by who?

***

Quan was sitting on the passenger side of the Dodge Charger, cradling the AK-47 assault rifle in his lap. He was having conflicted thoughts about what he had just done and what he thought he had seen in the process of the murder mission.

"I'm tellin' you, my nigga — that did look like young Zion back there," said Boogie, who was the second gunman sitting behind Quan in the back seat.

Quan shook his head in discernment. "I don't know, Boogie," he said.

"I'll tell you what. We can switch whips right now and go back and check it out. Or hit Dreka up and tell her to go round there."

"Dreka sounds about right," Tyreek interjected. "She can get there and check it out before twelve come and regulate shit," he said.

So Dreka it is, thought Quan, as he called the sister of one of his fellow soldiers. He just hoped that she was at the house to make her way around there. Because if it was Zion he had seen tonight, he was going to lose his mental.

It was bad enough he had just ordered the murder of his woman. Yvonnie was becoming a liability, and he couldn't risk that. It was better to sacrifice her than allow her actions to sink the whole ship and lose all around the board.

"Hello?" Dreka answered on the second ring.

"This Quan," he said.

"I know who this is, boy," came Dreka's high-pitched tone of voice, obviously high by the slowness in which she spoke to him. "What you want, Quan? Because the only time you hit my number is whenever you want *Mz. Deep Throat*," she said. "Naw what?"

If one could see the look on his face.

Quan said, "Some shit just popped off around the way, and I need you to go check it out."

"We heard all those gunshots," she said. "Me and Tory on our way to go see what's going on right now." Dreka was indeed high — either on weed, or pills, or both.

"I'm lookin' for someone in particular."

"Who?"

"Zion," he replied. "The Golden Child."

"The boy who was said to have set you up—" she was saying before Quan cut her short.

"That's not true. It just a rumor. A misunderstanding of what really happened," he said.

There was a brief pause.

"So what really happened then, Quan?" she asked.

"I'll tell you after you go check it out for me," he told her and hung the phone up.

Quan knew she would hit back as soon as she made it to the location and looked for him.

A blunt was passed up front, and Quan accepted it in rotation. He didn't even hit the blunt two good times before his phone rang. He checked the display and thought it was Dreka calling back, but it was Ced that was trying to reach him.

"What it do, brah?"

"Go somewhere in public right now where you are seen," Ced replied.

"Somewhere public?" Quan said.

"No questions. Just do it, brah."

"A'ight."

The only public place Quan thought it was best to be at a time like this was the local KFC chicken joint. He and Boogie went inside while Tyreek remained out the door scoping the scene and staying on point.

Boogie was actually in line to order food when the call came through from Dreka. He slid into a table booth to take the call, placing himself in the view of the establishment's video surveillance.

Whatever it was Ced was up to, he wanted Quan around people who'd alibi him in case some bullshit was part of the game. Ced was securing his position.

"Talk to me," he answered Dreka's call.

"It's ugly out here, baby. But no, he's not there. Only Loony, Preach, Jarvis, Lil' One, and that markass busta Zip."

"Are you sure that's everybody?"

"That's everybody, baby."

Quan looked up at the entrance door as a female and two young children entered.

"Thank you, Dee. I'll hit you back later," he said.

"I thought—"

He hung the line up on her and could see Dreka cussing his ass out for hanging up on her a second time. But she couldn't call back — Dreka was too preoccupied with what was going on around her to even care.

Another eight minutes later, Boogie slid into the booth across from Quan with a box of chicken in front of him. Quan looked at him and the box of food and wondered if he could even eat anything at all at that moment.

"So what's the verdict?"

"It wasn't Lil' Zy," Quan said.

"Good," said Boogie. "'Cause I know you woulda never forgave yourself if it was."

"Never," he agreed.

And it wouldn't be the first time.

Chapter 20

Now that the mission was done, all Zion wanted was to be with his loved ones, so he asked Rashia to drop him back off at the hospital where his presence was being awaited. Before reaching that point, Rashia had taken the side route from Friendship to Lake Skillet where Jabo wanted to be dropped off. He had to go home before it was way too late and his parents got on his case about blowing curfew again.

Jabo was seventeen years old, dedicated to being a certified player in the street games, and tonight paved that way for him. However, it wasn't gonna be easy now, because he was bound to be tested on every corner. Jabo had to earn his keep now. He was destined.

Meanwhile, Rashia and Zion talked that talk as they rode through traffic. She got to really know Zion Griffen tonight besides what she read in the sports column in the paper online. Not only had she witnessed his inner beast tonight, but learned of him as a true person. Zion was not a street nigga from a long shot; he was just forced into a bad situation where his loyalty was tested. Zion was loyal to a fault. He indeed was a sweetheart, and Rashia wished he never had to go through this.

Then he told her about Candice again, but this time outlining his love for her in a way only a person whose love is pure would understand. She understood exactly how he felt.

Rashia wanted so bad to share with him what she experienced today as well. She felt like she could share just about anything with Zion, and he would not look at her any differently. He wouldn't judge her.

At the hospital, Zion decided to go see Oscar first because he knew by now his brother was beside himself with worry. It was so like Oscar to put his own personal manners aside just to make sure his brother was all right. Upon entering the room, Zion was caught off guard by the presence of his Aunt Cathy — Kelli's mother and one of the few women he disliked in his family. Cathy was one of those women who thought she had all the sense, always talking down on the next person like she was better than everybody else. The only way he tolerated her was because of Kelli, who too couldn't stand her own mother at times.

This situation was different this time because Kelli was dead, and Zion knew he had to be gentle with his mother's sister. Aunt Cathy was grieving, and she needed all the love she could get. Hell, they all were grieving in their own way — some much more ridiculous than others.

"Zion!" Tabitha bolted from her chair next to Oscar's bed and hurried over to her son, pulling him into her arms. "You had me so worried."

"We all were," included Lex, stepping over to lay a hand upon his shoulder.

Also included in the room, besides the patient, was one of Oscar's sidekicks in the streets — and of course, Joya, with her emotional ass. They all were part of the same circle of grief and undeniable fear of what might happen next.

"How my brotha doing?" asked Zion.

"He'd just about drove us all up the wall worrying about your ass, Zee." This came from Peggie, looking worse for wear at that moment.

After embracing his Aunt Cathy and telling her how sorry he was about Kelli dying, he then whispered in her ear, "*Her death has been avenged, auntie. She can rest forever in peace now*."

That made the woman cry, and she turned into her sister's embrace and sobbed her heart out. It wasn't so much the aspect of her daughter's killers being dead, but the tone in which Zion had used. She knew without a shadow of a doubt this wasn't the same boy she watched grow up for the past eighteen years.

Zion was a killer. It was laden in his voice — she sensed it all over his person. That's what scared her so, that her nephew had gone and become ruined. Zion had a darkness now. The Golden Child was no longer there anymore, for he had been replaced by a killer.

With a nonchalant shrug, Zion moved over to his brother's bedside and just stood there watching him sleep for a minute.

"Wake up, fat boy!" Zion nudged him awake, pushing a hand against his meaty shoulder.

Slowly but surely, Oscar's eyes fluttered open from his drug-induced coma, then he stared up at Zion for a short moment.

"Zee?"

"I'm right here, bro. It's me," he said.

"What's the score?" Oscar asked groggily.

That's when Zion leaned down to his brother's ear and whispered to him something that made Oscar's eyes widen.

"We winning, then. Good," said Oscar, and then he went back under again, falling asleep with a wicked smirk on his face.

Zion smirked back at him, but in his heart of hearts, he knew he had fucked up somehow — and that had him scared. It was only natural.

***

Having gone through enough bullshit for one day, Rashia wanted to go home and get herself together. Maybe drink a glass of wine, smoke her an occasional joint, and take a nice hot shower before hopping in bed. She needed some alone time to herself. She would go back and visit her grandmother in the morning. For now Hazel had her beloved Hank watching over her. The man was a godsend, and Rashia was so grateful of him. Hazel had a winner in him. He was a fool for her and her pretty brown eyes.

Pulling up into the parking space outside her apartment building, Rashia felt her stomach growl with need of nutrition. Maybe she would fix up a couple of *Hot Pockets* while she was at it. That'll put her right in her place of comfort. She couldn't wait to get inside. She was exhausted. Opening the car door, Rashia cussed under her breath about getting the driver door fixed. She would make Donte pay for it since it was his men that broke it in the first place.

Rashia climbed out of the car just as a dark figure came to stand in her path along the sidewalk between both parked cars. She shut the car door and that's when another lone dark figure appeared at the rear of both cars. Immediately Rashia sensed danger as she placed her back against her car door.

"The fuck you niggas want, huh!" she hissed at them, looking from one to the other.

The one at the rear of the car struck first, rushing in on Rashia and started laying hands on her, but she wasn't no chump. Rashia fought that nigga back. She refused to be cowered by the likes of two niggas. Then the second one joined in and together they got on her ass. That didn't last long before she fought for possession of the pistol she had tucked. She sacrificed herself to obtain the weapon, and when she did, she let that muthafucka bang. The first shot went into the nigga's leg causing him to cry out, which made the other cease his actions. Then Rashia shot him again, but this time in the face. That was all the indication the other needed to make a run for it.

"Don't run now!' growled Rashia, aiming the pistol and sending two shots his way.

Then she stepped over the dead man slumped between both cars to take chase after him, but he only ran so far before another shadowy figure stepped out of nowhere and shot him dead in the chest. This stunned Rashia for a second, but then she rushed forward to come face to face with the person who aided her.

"Do what you do," he said.

Rashia glared down at the man at her feet who was still breathing but not for along before his death wiped him out. She squeezed the trigger and put one in his head before the weapon slammed empty.

Click. She pulled trigger again.

Click.

"It's over," he said.

She looked up at Killah oddly, then she snatched his gun away and dumped four shots into the body at their feet.

"Now it's over," she said.

"We gotta go now, Rashia."

"We?" she regarded him cautiously.

He nodded. "It's not safe for you here tonight. We need to go like right now."

"Who was these niggaz?" Rashia asked.

"I'll tell you in the car," he said.

Then, without another word, Killah turned on his heels and walked away. Reluctantly, she followed after him as people stepped out of their dark apartments or peeked out of their windows to see what all the fuss was about.

A minute later, Rashia was sitting alongside of Donte's most trusted good and closest friend. For a long minute Killah didn't say a word until he felt as though they were at a safer distance away from the bloody crime scene.

"I'm listening," said Rashia.

"Those guys back there was both of Donte's men, but he didn't authorize that shit."

"Then who did? You?" Rashia gripped tightly of the new gun she was now in possession of.

"If I authorized it Rashia, why would I kill my own man?" he questioned.

"Because he tucked his tail and ran like a bitch. Or maybe to manipulatively convince me you're on my side so that you can kill me yourself. Or maybe the same reason you stood by and watched them niggaz jump on me and didn't bother to stop it," she replied.

"All of those were great points, Rashia, but neither one of them were any of my intentions."

"Then what are your intentions?"

"To save you."

"To save me?" she frowned. "From what?"

"It's not about from what but from whom," Killah told her with a hint of suspicion.

"Who?"

He paused for effect.

"Elijah Green. Fifteen years ago. You tried to save his life and damn near lost yours in the process. Now the universe wants to compensate you for your actions all those years ago."

"Compensate me how?" she asked.

"I guess we'll cross that bridge when we get there," he said. "Now sit back and relax."

Chapter 21

The next two hours were crucial. The authorities were out on the town raising pure hell, and some were gratified with the latest news. Detective Bo Henderson had been snatched. Witnesses said they saw Bo enter the liquor store downtown to purchase his usual — a bottle of Crown Royal. Then, upon him exiting the liquor store, headed back to his car, a team of gunmen surrounded him in the parking lot. Then he was snatched up and dragged into the trunk of a car and driven off.

Instantly, the authorities went for Quan about it, and his alibi stood firm. He was in the KFC eating wingless BBQ chicken and biscuits when the abduction took place. Quan was already expecting them to show up, so he placed himself where they could easily spot him and confront him, just so he could get the bullshit out the way. No one knew where Bo was taken. It was a mystery. Even Quan didn't know — and it was by his order that Bo was even gone. He just hoped that wherever Bo was taken, he doesn't pop back up.

When the news of Bo's kidnap got around to the families of those with whom he had hurt or assumed killed — and all the street niggaz he had troubled over the years — they all celebrated.

The boogieman has been slain. Bo Henderson was no more.

"I wonder who's gonna step up and take his place now," said Melodi.

"Nobody," said Zion.

"Bo was considered the worst of the worst. Nobody will be stupid enough to fill in those shoes at the risk of being killed too," said Melodi, sitting across from him in the hospital cafeteria, where Candice had been transported to Tallahassee Memorial Hospital to be in the care of the best doctors in the area.

The Quincy Hospital was just too small for the injuries, and the condition Candice was in. The transportation notice had come out of the blue, and she was flown there by helicopter and landed an hour ago. This scared Zion, and he wanted to be present in case he was needed somehow. He felt if he left her side again without her waking up and seeing him, something bad would happen. Zion had never been so frightened in his life. Scared that the girl he truly loved would die before he could give her love.

"You need to get some rest," Zion said to Melodi, whose eyes looked glossy with exhaustion.

A tired smile formed on her face.

"I know. And so do you. You still got school tomorrow, or are you skipping it for a day or two?"

"School." Zion hadn't thought about school since he left that afternoon.

He then stood up and stepped around the table and reached for Melodi to help her to her feet.

"You wanna go see Candice now?"

"I want you to go back and get some sleep, Mz. Tired Eyez. You've been fightin' for the last hour. C'mon. Let's get you back to the room," he said, taking her by the elbow, and together they made the journey back to the room.

Upon entering the room, they both were taken aback by the unexpected presence that occupied its space. One look at the man, and Zion knew there was about to be some trouble.

"Why are you here, Kevin?" demanded Melodi.

The man shared the same high yellow skin tone as Candice, same face structure and all — evidence that he was her biological father.

"What the hell does it look like, Mel? I heard about what happened to my daughter, and I had to come out and see her," said Kevin Brown.

"You're not supposed to be here, Kevin."

"How come?"

"Because," she said, "you're a fugitive on the run. And if they find you here, that would make things bad on everybody." Her tone was sharp.

"But she's my daughter."

"And I must protect her from whatever that may cause further harm," she added. "Including you."

The look on Kevin's face was hard, as if he couldn't believe the shit he was hearing.

"Like you protected her from almost gettin' killed?" he retorted.

His words hurt her.

"That's enough." Zion stepped forward.

Kevin glared at him coldly. "And who the fuck are you, little nigga?"

"Zion Griffen," he said. "And I think it's best that you leave this room right now. Or else."

"Or else what, nigga?"

That's when Zion drew the gun and aimed it at the man's head.

"I see you think it's a game, man."

"Zee . . ." Melodi gasped.

"You're a fugitive on the run for two counts of murder. I can kill your ass right here now, and it'll be justified. I'll be doing the world a favor. You were the aggressor, you're America's Most Wanted, and one shot to the head is all it takes. Call my bluff, Mr. Big Mouth?" Zion held his position firmly, never breaking eye contact.

Swiveling his gaze over at the mother of his child, Kevin said, "So that's how it is?"

"It is what it is, Kevin," she shrugged.

With a grave nod of the head, Kevin shot one more glaring glance at Zion, pulled on his hat and shades, and took his leave. Seeing him go seemed to have knocked all the wind out of Melodi. She took a seat in the chair across from Candice's bed and leaned her weary head back and shut her eyes.

"I'm grateful for you, Zion," she said.

He just looked at her quietly.

"But you're a dangerous individual." Melodi continued with a yawn. "How did you become so dangerous?"

Before he could deliver a reply, Melodi was already asleep. Zion located an extra blanket and covered her. The woman was dead tired. She was finished, and Zion had just begun his transformation.

***

When morning came, it did so with great relief for Sheena. The tragedies of the evening before had knocked her off her square for a second, but she made up for it in the end. Losing Lyric yesterday was devastating, but Sheena had zero tolerance for betrayal. She didn't see that coming, though — not Lyric. It wasn't like she was hurting for money. Sheena was a hood-rich millionaire, worth about $2.1 million, and that was majority contract hits she'd done. She didn't live lavishly like that. Sheena preferred to still live in the trenches, and Lyric never really had to ask for nothing — only quality time with her woman. That's all Lyric ever asked for the most.

Why would she betray Zion, though? What had he done to her to make Lyric do what she did? It was a question that she no longer could get Lyric to answer because she was dead, but she intended on finding answers from Zion, if he had any. Which is why she made her way over to TMH sometime after nine that morning to go scoop him up.

It amazed Sheena to learn that after all Zion had gone through the day before, he still wanted to go to school that day — even if it was just for a little while. Zion gave her specific instructions on what he wanted, and she saw to it that it got done. Meaning fresh clothes and shoes, and his favorite G-Shock watch off his bedroom dresser top — if a crackhead hadn't witnessed the broken front door and snuck inside to ransack the place. Sheena collected what her dear cousin desired and brought it straight to him.

"Thanks," said Zion after putting on a fresh Ralph Lauren outfit and stepping his feet into a brand-new pair of cocaine-white Air Force 1s.

"No biggie," she said.

Zion then placed kisses up Candice's cheek, embraced her mother along with a kiss too, and promised to return later, and eventually took his leave. He looked well rested, but his eyes told a whole nother story. He had been crying again — crying over Candice, his brother, Kelli, and all his bad decisions, which getting in the car with Quan had caused.

Sheena decided to wait until they were on the road to confront Zion about Lyric, but by that time a call came through to her, and Sheena was quite astounded by the essence of the conversation.

"I got a mission for you," said Quan — the last person she wanted to talk to at the moment.

"The usual?" she asked.

"Of course."

"Send—"

"The details are already on you right now," he cut in, and Sheena felt the phone vibrate with the incoming text message.

She looked at the phone, activated the text message, and read it. Immediately, her eyes almost popped out of her head.

Sheena said, "Of all the thangz you could be asking me, brotha."

"Fifty bandz," said Quan.

"Sold. I'll get right on it."

"And Sheena?"

"Enough said, Quan. Bye. Love you." And then she hung up in his ear.

Sheena couldn't believe that Quan wanted her to take Tony out the game. He was his best friend, his brother, and for Quan to want him dead, he must have really crossed him. Betrayal. That seemed to be the norm nowadays — Lyric, Yvonnie, and now Tony. Where was the honor at when it shouldn't be hard to give?

"What did Quan want?" Zion asked.

"Confidential," she said.

He nodded.

"But I do have an important question for you, though, Zee," she added.

"Ask."

"Why would Lyric—"

"Why would Lyric betray me the way she did?" Zion stepped on top of her words.

He appeared as if he was giving it some thought.

"I've thought about that a hundred times since it happened, and I still don't know why she did it. I don't know, Sheena. I really don't know," he said.

Chapter 22

Trina parked her Mercedes-Benz in her reserved spot outside of *Crowns Hair & Nail Salon.* She looked up and saw Block, Tre, and Raine standing outside the front entrance of the building. The shop didn't open until nine o'clock, and from the looks of it, the place was already swinging. Something wasn't right here, and Trina was determined to see what it was. Nobody should be opening the doors of her salon but her.

Trina grabbed her purse and got out of the car, heading straight for the building entrance. Strangely, when they saw her coming, both Block and Raine stepped in her path, blocking the doors. She kept right on pushing until Raine stiff-armed her into a halt.

"The fuck are you doing, bitch?" Trina hissed.

"You can't enter the shop."

"What? This is my fuckin' salon!" she bristled.

"I only got my orders not to let you go inside the building," said Block.

"Orders from who, nigga?" Trina snapped.

"Who else?"

Donte. Trina knew it had to be Donte. Who else would call that type of shot? This made Trina so mad she made an attempt to bulldoze through them to get to the door, but Block was too big of a nigga to just let that happen.

"It's my goddamn salon!" she screamed.

"Not anymore, bitch!" said Raine, cracking her knuckles in preparation to throw some hands.

Trina was on the verge of blowing up, and Raine was going to knock her ass back down.

"You know . . .?" Trina reached inside her purse for her phone.

She was about to call Donte herself and get to the bottom of the situation. Tre was the silent assassin type, but he was trustworthy and always on point when you needed him to be. Before Trina could hit Donte's number on speed dial, he had already made the connection on his own cellular.

"I got Donte right here," offered Tre, extending the phone towards her.

Trina paused and growled at him, then she reached out and snatched the phone away from him.

"Hello?"

"What, cuz?" Donte sounded annoyed.

"Did you ban me from my salon?" she responded.

"First off, *Crowns* is my salon, so let's get that clear. I only allowed you to manage it. And secondly, you are not to enter the salon unless you are a customer. Yeah. You played yourself outta pocket yesterday, and now you gotta deal wit' the loss, cuz," said Donte.

"But what did I do wrong?" she asked, sounding like she was about to cry.

"You used my name to convince my men to follow your orders, and now they're dead. That shit was totally unacceptable in my book."

That was the blow Trina wasn't expecting to take, but when it hit, it impacted hard. He was talking about the two niggas she sent after Rashia last night—Lucky and Walt.

"They're dead?"

"What the fuck you think, Trina!" Donte wanted to spazz out on her, but instead, he hung up the phone in her ear.

"Hello? Donte?" she spoke into the receiver. "Hello!" Trina frowned. "Well, fuck you then!" She was about to throw the phone until Tre restrained her arm and took it away from her.

"Now that you got the words from the man himself," Raine replied. "Step in or get stepped on, Trina."

"Who did he put in charge?" she asked.

"None of your fuckin' business."

Trina wanted to scream. She then nodded with an evil glint in her eyes.

"You just watch and see," Trina said. "Donte gonna wish he never crossed a bitch like me."

"Is that a threat?" Block replied.

"It's a fact, nigga." Then Trina hurried off to her Benz and got in.

She then peeled away from the salon with screeching tires. She was livid with her cousin Donte. Her last move was what did it. Another sad ending. If only Trina had kept her fucking mouth shut.

***

When the recess bell rang, Zion yawned and stood up from the table of his Biology class with Mr. Richard Rosenburg. Today, he wasn't carrying a backpack—only his gun and a heavy burden on his broad shoulders.

Since his arrival this morning on campus, he'd been the center of attention. Everybody had questions about the rumors, the murders—including Candice's situation—and what he was going to do about Jamir, De'Kari, and Duke. Most of the questions came from those in his neighborhood, the ones who personally witnessed the tragedies on their own turf.

Zion ignored everybody who asked about the situation rather than asked about his well-being. He was kicking himself in the ass by third period for ever deciding to show up. He had more serious shit on his plate than catering to the curiosities of the people. Zion had a headache. This wasn't the way he wanted to spend his Friday. Actually, he didn't plan on spending the whole day at school. He and Oscar had made plans to head over to Tallahassee, where the Upward Bound Senior students from all over the two counties were to be attending the college campuses of FAMU and Florida State University. He wasn't part of the Upward Bound program, but he and Oscar thought it would be cool to show up anyway.

Oscar dropped out of school two years ago. He was a student of hard knocks, the class of the trenches, and a scholar of the street game. Oscar was very intelligent, would be graduating too if only he had stayed in school—but Oscar was Oscar, and you had to love him still. He was the prince of hoodlums.

He was next in line to be one of the most respected and feared men in the streets.

Upon his exit of the classroom, Zion was met in the hallway by three others: Kahleel Pittman, the star quarterback; DJ Price, the vicious cornerback; and the team's rookie strong safety, Shamar Sanders. These were Zion's athletic brothers, his everyday crew while at school, and a force to be reckoned with on the football field.

The brothers all dapped Zion up, and they embraced one another. Still, all eyes were on Zion, and he ignored them for the undivided attention of his teammates.

"Heard you stopped by the hospital last night," Zion said to Kahleel, another senior who had already gotten accepted at University of Miami.

"Yeah," said Kahleel. "I had to see you, bro. But I saw Oscar and your mom."

The crew were bypassing everybody milling through the hall toward the exit doors. DJ walked in front of Zion, obviously clearing the path for them. Shamar was the sophomore of the crew, but they treated him equally. The others were seniors and bound to leave him behind, but Shamar had shown that he was ready to tote the torch alone. He had great potential.

During this time of day, some students would leave campus to go out and eat or do whatever it is they did during recess, while others filled the school's cafeteria or just roamed around doing shit until the next bell rang. The teammates were all deciding what they wanted to do when, all of a sudden, Heather popped up out of nowhere.

"Can I steal you away for a while?" Heather was looking good in her tight-fitted Fendi-washed denim jeans and high-top sneakers.

"Yes, you can," Shamar shoved Zion forward, and that made DJ smirk.

"My man," said Kahleel with a grin.

Heather's presence had all the boys eyeing her with lust, and the girls with quiet envy and attitudes that she so easily captured the attention of the very same boys they liked.

"Thank you, boys," Heather sang to them, and Shamar was smitten by her beauty.

"Y'all are some real traitors!" Zion called out to his brothers as Heather draped her arm around his shoulders and guided him away.

"I'm taking you away from here," she said.

"Why?"

"Because," she said, "something even more amazing awaits your presence, Zee."

"Candice?" he said with hope in his eyes.

"Nope."

"Then what's amazing?" he wondered.

"You'll see when we get there."

"Where is there?"

Heather laughed out loud. "You know, you ask too many gotdamn questions—you should be a lawyer or something," she teased him.

From there, Heather led him to her car parked out front before the school and drove him away. The whole time, Zion questioned her about where they were going. Heather stuck to her guns and just told him to be patient.

"Trust me, Zee, it'll be worth the wait," Heather said with open clarity.

Not long afterward, they had entered Lake Skillet and turned onto Hamilton Street when it finally registered where they were going. She was taking him home—to his house—but why? he wondered with soundless curiosity.

"You brought me home," he said.

"Yep. Now c'mon, Zee!" Heather opened the door and got out.

She beckoned him with a wave, and Zion slowly removed himself from the car. He had to survey his surroundings first before he allowed himself to get out.

As Zion made his way toward his house, he noticed there was a new front door in place. Then that same front door opened, and there stood his mother. In her hand, she gripped a bottle of champagne. The expression on her face was worth a thousand promises.

"What's going on, Mama?" he asked as he climbed the steps up to come face to face with his mother.

"Come," she said, taking him by the hand and guiding him over the threshold into the house.

It was then that Zion saw Sheena, Quan, his Uncle David, Matilda, and Lex. He looked for any telltale sign of just why he was pulled away from school, and that's when Tabitha reached to pluck up the standard mailing envelope from the coffee table before them. His mother handed him the envelope, and Zion felt his heart lurch with unmistakable surprise. It was the envelope's stamp of the addressee that made him stop and take a breather.

"Open it," Quan replied.

"Shut up, Q!" Sheena nudged him, having already completed half of the mission he had presented to her earlier.

It so happened that Tony never did take that trip to Memphis—he'd been close to home all along. Unfortunately for him, Tony had exposed his hand through Bo's testimony after the confession was tortured out of him. The detective had given up everything, anything, just so the pain would stop. He gave up Tony. In return, Tony gave up his life.

Zion opened the envelope.

"It's from Georgia State," he said excitedly. "Dear Zion Griffen. Thank you for applying to our administration, and I am pleased to say that you have been accepted on a full athletic scholarship with our football program . . ." Zion's voice cracked with emotion as his eyes filled with tears.

Then he bowed his head and said, "We made it."

Tabitha was crying openly now. "Yes, we did, baby boy. We made it!" She hugged him.

Zion cried too. After all the universe threw his way the day before, he still prevailed. He got just what he worked so hard to accomplish—and that was a chance to go to college and play for his favorite college team, the Georgia Bulldogs. Now that was a blessing to be thankful for.

Epilogue

Another blessing walked through the front door of the condo apartment Rashia had been taken to just the night before, and that blessing was none other than the man she already knew—Donte.

At the sight of him, Rashia was instantly reminded of the hell he took her through just the day before, but for some reason, she could not be mad at him. Rashia knew the game and respected it for what it was.

When Donte walked through that door, she didn't spazz out on him. Rashia just kept right on eating her bowl of strawberries and whipped cream in questioning silence. In his hand, Donte carried a yellow gift bag that swung from his grip solidly. He approached the section where she sat upon the plush sofa in the large living room. To her astonishment, Donte eased himself down onto the sofa directly across from her.

"What's in the bag?" she asked.

"Your future," he answered.

The statement made her cease all actions.

"My future? How is that possible?"

Donte reached into the bag for the first two items, which were a set of keys and what appeared to be paper documents.

"Let's just say *Crowns Hair & Nail Salon* deserves to have a better owner than its current one," said Donte with a straight face.

"Owner? Who?" she replied.

"Well, you of course. The deed has been drawn up and is ready for your signature. Here's the keys to your new salon."

Donte tossed her the keys, and Rashia caught them gracefully.

"Next," Donte removed the next item, which was another key. "Here's the key to your new condo as well. Be sure to remember there's a wall safe behind the master bedroom medicine cabinet with a million dollars in cash in it."

"A million dollars!" Rashia almost choked on the fruit she was eating.

"That's not all," he told her.

"What else could there be, Donte?" Rashia was totally baffled by all this.

"My heart," he replied and stood up. Then he stepped around the table to face her head-on. "I give you my heart, Rashia. Because that boy you tried to save and took bullets for fifteen years ago?"

Donte took her hand in his.

She closed her eyes. "Elijah," she whispered.

"That was my baby brotha, Rashia," he said. "And for that loyalty, this is the price you get. A new shot at life. A better one—for you and your beautiful grandmother," he exclaimed humbly.

That's what did it for her.

He wanted what's best for Hazel. Her pride and joy.

Lock Down Publications and Ca$h Presents Assisted Publishing Packages

Due to an increase in the price of services we have increased our prices. The prices below reflect the price increase as of 11/1/24.

BASIC PACKAGE **$699** Editing Cover Design Formatting	**UPGRADED PACKAGE** **$1000** Typing Editing Cover Design Formatting Upload eBooks to Amazon Upload Paperback to Amazon
ADVANCE PACKAGE **$1,400** Typing Editing (line editing/content) Cover Design Formatting Copyright Registration Proofreading Upload eBooks to Amazon Upload Paperback to Amazon	**LDP SUPREME PACKAGE** **$1,700** Typing Editing (line editing/content) Cover Design Formatting Copyright Registration Proofreading Set up Amazon Account Upload eBooks to Amazon Upload Paperback to Amazon Advertise on LDP's Amazon and Facebook Page

***

Other services available upon request.
Additional charges may apply

Lock Down Publications
P.O. Box 944
Stockbridge, GA 30281-9998
Phone: 470 303-9761
Email: lockdownpublications@gmail.com

Submission Guideline

Submit the first three chapters of your completed manuscript to ldpsubmissions@gmail.com. In the subject line add **Your Book's Title**. The manuscript must be in a Word Doc file and sent as an attachment. Document should be in Times New Roman, double spaced, and in size 12 font. Also, provide your synopsis and full contact information. If sending multiple submissions, they must each be in a separate email.

Have a story but no way to send it electronically? You can still submit to LDP/Ca$h Presents. Send in the first three chapters, written or typed, of your completed manuscript to:

LDP: Submissions Dept
P.O. Box 944
Stockbridge, GA 30281-9998

DO NOT send original manuscript. Must be a duplicate. Provide your synopsis and a cover letter containing your full contact information.

Thanks for considering LDP and Ca$h Presents.

NEW RELEASES

BLOODLINE OF A SAVAGE 1-3
THESE VICIOUS STREETS 1-3
RELENTLESS GOON 1-3
BY PRINCE A. TAUHID

THE BUTTERFLY MAFIA 1-3
BY FUMIYA PAYNE

A THUG'S STREET PRINCESS 1&2
BY MEESHA

CITY OF SMOKE 3
BY MOLOTTI

GET IT IN SLUGS 1 &2
BY B. STALL

STANDING ON HER BUSINESS 1&2
BY DG SANTANA

STEPPERS 1,2&3
THE REAL BADDIES OF CHI-RAQ
BY KING RIO

THE LANE 1&2
BY KEN-KEN SPENCE

THUG OF SPADES 1&2
LOVE IN THE TRENCHES 2
CORNER BOYS
BY COREY ROBINSON

TIL DEATH 3
BY ARYANNA

SECURE DA BAG | IRA B.

THE BIRTH OF A GANGSTER 4
BY DELMONT PLAYER

PRODUCT OF THE STREETS 1-3
BY DEMOND "MONEY" ANDERSON

NO TIME FOR ERROR
BY KEESE

MONEY HUNGRY DEMONS 1-2
BY TRANAY ADAMS

HUB CITY MENACE 1-3
BY J. WHITE

A THUGGISH PASSION 1&2
LAND OF DA HOOLIGANZ 1-4
KILLAZ ON STANDBY 1&2
BY IRA B.

FO'EVA ROLLIN 1&2
BY ASSA RAYMOND BAKER

THE LEVEL UP 1&3
BY LUXURY KING

Coming Soon from Lock Down Publications/Ca$h Presents

IF YOU CROSS ME ONCE 6
ANGEL V
By Anthony Fields

A THUGS STREET PRINCESS 3
By Meesha

CORNER BOYS 2
By Corey Robinson

THA TAKEOVER
By Keith Chandler

BETRAYAL OF A G 2
By Ray Vinci

SAVAGE FAMILY EMPIRE 1&2
SOULLESS GOON 1,2&3
THE DIRTY SIDE OF MONEY 1,2&3
By Prince

FOR MY ENEMY'S SAKE
AMBITIONS OF A SLIDER
FRESH OFF DA PORCH
By IRA B.

BY THE TRUCKLOAD 1-4
TIPPIN' THE SCALES 1-3
BAD BITCHES WIT GUNZ 3
PROBLEM SOLVED 2
By Christopher "Diesel" Hornezes

Available Now

RESTRAINING ORDER 1 & 2
By **CA$H & Coffee**

LOVE KNOWS NO BOUNDARIES 1-3
By **Coffee**

RAISED AS A GOON I, II, III & IV
BRED BY THE SLUMS I, II, III
BLAST FOR ME I & II
ROTTEN TO THE CORE I II III
A BRONX TALE I, II, III
DUFFLE BAG CARTEL I II III IV V VI
HEARTLESS GOON I II III IV V
A SAVAGE DOPEBOY I II
DRUG LORDS I II III
CUTTHROAT MAFIA I II
KING OF THE TRENCHES
By **Ghost**

LAY IT DOWN I & II
LAST OF A DYING BREED I II
BLOOD STAINS OF A SHOTTA I & II III
By **Jamaica**

LOYAL TO THE GAME I II III
LIFE OF SIN I, II III
By **TJ & Jelissa**

IF LOVING HIM IS WRONG…I & II
LOVE ME EVEN WHEN IT HURTS I II III
By **Jelissa**

PUSH IT TO THE LIMIT
By **Bre' Hayes**

SECURE DA BAG | IRA B.

BLOODY COMMAS I & II
SKI MASK CARTEL I, II & III
KING OF NEW YORK I II, III IV V
RISE TO POWER I II III
COKE KINGS I II III IV V
BORN HEARTLESS I II III IV
KING OF THE TRAP I II
By **T.J. Edwards**

WHEN THE STREETS CLAP BACK I & II III
THE HEART OF A SAVAGE I II III IV
MONEY MAFIA I II
LOYAL TO THE SOIL I II III
By **Jibril Williams**

A DISTINGUISHED THUG STOLE MY HEART I II & III
LOVE SHOULDN'T HURT I II III IV
RENEGADE BOYS 1-4
PAID IN KARMA 1-3
SAVAGE STORMS 1-3
AN UNFORESEEN LOVE 1-3
BABY, I'M WINTERTIME COLD 1-3
A THUG'S STREET PRINCESS 1&2
By **Meesha**

A GANGSTER'S CODE 1-3
A GANGSTER'S SYN 1-3
THE SAVAGE LIFE 1-3
CHAINED TO THE STREETS 1-3
BLOOD ON THE MONEY 1-3
A GANGSTA'S PAIN 1-3
BEAUTIFUL LIES AND UGLY TRUTHS
CHURCH IN THESE STREETS
By **J-Blunt**

CUM FOR ME 1-8
An LDP Erotica Collaboration

SECURE DA BAG | IRA B.

BLOOD OF A BOSS 1-5
SHADOWS OF THE GAME
TRAP BASTARD
By **Askari**

THE STREETS BLEED MURDER 1-3
THE HEART OF A GANGSTA 1-3
By **Jerry Jackson**

WHEN A GOOD GIRL GOES BAD
By **Adrienne**

THE COST OF LOYALTY 1-3
By **Kweli**

BRIDE OF A HUSTLA 1-3
THE FETTI GIRLS 1-3
CORRUPTED BY A GANGSTA 1-4
BLINDED BY HIS LOVE
THE PRICE YOU PAY FOR LOVE 1-3
DOPE GIRL MAGIC 1-3
By **Destiny Skai**

A KINGPIN'S AMBITION
A KINGPIN'S AMBITION II
I MURDER FOR THE DOUGH
By **Ambitious**

TRUE SAVAGE 1-7
DOPE BOY MAGIC 1-3
MIDNIGHT CARTEL 1-3
CITY OF KINGZ 1&2
NIGHTMARE ON SILENT AVE
THE PLUG OF LIL MEXICO 1&2
CLASSIC CITY
By **Chris Green**

A GANGSTER'S REVENGE 1-4
THE BOSS MAN'S DAUGHTERS 1-5
A SAVAGE LOVE 1&2
BAE BELONGS TO ME 1&2
A HUSTLER'S DECEIT 1-3
WHAT BAD BITCHES DO 1-3
SOUL OF A MONSTER 1-3
KILL ZONE
A DOPE BOY'S QUEEN 1-3
TIL DEATH 1-3
IMMA DIE BOUT MINE 1-6
DYING FOR LIKES
By **Aryanna**

A DOPEBOY'S PRAYER
By **Eddie "Wolf" Lee**

THE KING CARTEL 1-3
By **Frank Gresham**

THESE NIGGAS AIN'T LOYAL 1-3
By **Nikki Tee**

GANGSTA SHYT 1-3
By **CATO**

THE ULTIMATE BETRAYAL
By **Phoenix**

BOSS'N UP 1-3
By **Royal Nicole**

I LOVE YOU TO DEATH
By **Destiny J**

I RIDE FOR MY HITTA
I STILL RIDE FOR MY HITTA
By **Misty Holt**

LOVE & CHASIN' PAPER
By **Qay Crockett**

TO DIE IN VAIN
SINS OF A HUSTLA
By **ASAD**

BROOKLYN HUSTLAZ
By **Boogsy Morina**

BROOKLYN ON LOCK 1 & 2
By **Sonovia**

GANGSTA CITY
By **Teddy Duke**

A DRUG KING AND HIS DIAMOND 1-3
A DOPEMAN'S RICHES
HER MAN, MINE'S TOO 1&2
CASH MONEY HO'S
THE WIFEY I USED TO BE 1&2
PRETTY GIRLS DO NASTY THINGS
By **Nicole Goosby**

LIPSTICK KILLAH 1-3
CRIME OF PASSION 1-3
FRIEND OR FOE 1-3
By **Mimi**

TRAPHOUSE KING 1-3
KINGPIN KILLAZ 1-3
STREET KINGS 1&2
PAID IN BLOOD 1&2
CARTEL KILLAZ 1-3
DOPE GODS 1&2
By **Hood Rich**

THE STREETS ARE CALLING
By **Duquie Wilson**

STEADY MOBBN' 1-3
THE STREETS STAINED MY SOUL 1-3
By **Marcellus Allen**

WHO SHOT YA 1-3
SON OF A DOPE FIEND 1-4
HEAVEN GOT A GHETTO 1&2
SKI MASK MONEY 1&2
By **Renta**

GORILLAZ IN THE BAY 1-4
TEARS OF A GANGSTA 1/&2
3X KRAZY 1&2
STRAIGHT BEAST MODE 1&2
By **DE'KARI**

TRIGGADALE 1-3
MURDA WAS THE CASE 1-3
By **Elijah R. Freeman**

SLAUGHTER GANG 1-3
RUTHLESS HEART 1-3
By **Willie Slaughter**

GOD BLESS THE TRAPPERS 1-3
THESE SCANDALOUS STREETS 1-3
FEAR MY GANGSTA 1-5
THESE STREETS DON'T LOVE NOBODY 1-2
BURY ME A G 1-5
A GANGSTA'S EMPIRE 1-4
THE DOPEMAN'S BODYGAURD 1&2
THE REALEST KILLAZ 1-3
THE LAST OF THE OGS 1-3
By **Tranay Adams**

MARRIED TO A BOSS 1-3
By **Destiny Skai & Chris Green**

KINGZ OF THE GAME 1-7
CRIME BOSS 1-4
By **Playa Ray**

FUK SHYT
By **Blakk Diamond**

DON'T F#CK WITH MY HEART 1&2
By **Linnea**

ADDICTED TO THE DRAMA 1-3
IN THE ARM OF HIS BOSS
By **Jamila**

LOYALTY AIN'T PROMISED 1&2
By **Keith Williams**

YAYO 1-4
A SHOOTER'S AMBITION 1&2
BRED IN THE GAME
By **S. Allen**

TRAP GOD 1-3
RICH $AVAGE 1-3
MONEY IN THE GRAVE 1-3
CARTEL MONEY 1&2
By **Martell Troublesome Bolden**

FOREVER GANGSTA 1&2
GLOCKS ON SATIN SHEETS 1&2
By **Adrian Dulan**

TOE TAGZ 1-4
LEVELS TO THIS SHYT 1&2
IT'S JUST ME AND YOU
By **Ah'Million**

SECURE DA BAG | IRA B.

KINGPIN DREAMS 1-3
RAN OFF ON DA PLUG
By **Paper Boi Rari**

THE STREETS MADE ME 1-3
By **Larry D. Wright**

CONFESSIONS OF A GANGSTA 1-4
CONFESSIONS OF A JACKBOY 1-3
CONFESSIONS OF A HITMAN
CONFESSIONS OF A DOPE BOY
By **Nicholas Lock**

I'M NOTHING WITHOUT HIS LOVE
SINS OF A THUG
TO THE THUG I LOVED BEFORE
A GANGSTA SAVED XMAS
IN A HUSTLER I TRUST
By **Monet Dragun**

QUIET MONEY 1-3
THUG LIFE 1-3
EXTENDED CLIP 1&2
A GANGSTA'S PARADISE
By **Trai'Quan**

CAUGHT UP IN THE LIFE 1-3
THE STREETS NEVER LET GO 1-3
By **Robert Baptiste**

NEW TO THE GAME 1-3
MONEY, MURDER & MEMORIES 1-3
By **Malik D. Rice**

CREAM 2-3
THE STREETS WILL TALK
By **Yolanda Moore**

THE STREETS WILL NEVER CLOSE 1-3
By **K'ajji**

LIFE OF A SAVAGE 1-4
A GANGSTA'S QUR'AN 1-4
MURDA SEASON 1-3
GANGLAND CARTEL 1-3
CHI'RAQ GANGSTAS 1-4
KILLERS ON ELM STREET 1-3
JACK BOYZ N DA BRONX 1-3
A DOPEBOY'S DREAM 1-3
JACK BOYS VS DOPE BOYS 1-3
COKE GIRLZ
COKE BOYS
SOSA GANG 1&2
BRONX SAVAGES
BODYMORE KINGPINS
BLOOD OF A GOON
By **Romell Tukes**

CONCRETE KILLA 1-3
VICIOUS LOYALTY 1-3
BLOODY MONEY BAGS
By **Kingpen**

THE ULTIMATE SACRIFICE 1-6
KHADIFI
IF YOU CROSS ME ONCE 1-3
ANGEL 1-4
IN THE BLINK OF AN EYE
By **Anthony Fields**

THE LIFE OF A HOOD STAR
By **Ca$h & Rashia Wilson**

NIGHTMARES OF A HUSTLA 1-3
BLOOD AND GAMES 1&2
By **King Dream**

GHOST MOB
By **Stilloan Robinson**

HARD AND RUTHLESS 1&2
MOB TOWN 251
THE BILLIONAIRE BENTLEYS 1-3
REAL G'S MOVE IN SILENCE
By **Von Diesel**

MOB TIES 1-7
SOUL OF A HUSTLER, HEART OF A KILLER 1-3
GORILLAZ IN THE TRENCHES
OOPS CRY TOO 1&2
THE DAUGHTER OF A CARTEL BOSS
By **SayNoMore**

BODYMORE MURDERLAND 1-3
THE BIRTH OF A GANGSTER 1-4
By **Delmont Player**

FOR THE LOVE OF A BOSS 1&2
By **C. D. Blue**

KILLA KOUNTY 1-5
TENDER
By **Khufu**

MOBBED UP 1-4
THE BRICK MAN 1-5
THE COCAINE PRINCESS 1-10
STEPPERS 1-3
SUPER GREMLIN 1-4
A GANGSTA'S SON
By **King Rio**

MONEY GAME 1&2
By **Smoove Dolla**

SECURE DA BAG | IRA B.

A GANGSTA'S KARMA 1-5
By **FLAME**

KING OF THE TRENCHES 1-3
By **GHOST & TRANAY ADAMS**

BAD BITCHES WIT GUNZ 1&2
PROBLEM SOLVED
By "Christopher Diesel" Hornezes

QUEEN OF THE ZOO 1&2
By **Black Migo**

GRIMEY WAYS 1-3
BETRAYAL OF A G
By **Ray Vinci**

XMAS WITH AN ATL SHOOTER
By **Ca$h & Destiny Skai**

KING KILLA 1&2
By **Vincent "Vitto" Holloway**

BETRAYAL OF A THUG 1&2
By **Fre$h**

COUNTDOWN OF A KILLA 1&2
SEX, MURDER AND GOD 1&2
GUNS DOWN, BOTTOMS UP 1&2
By Lo-Life

THE MURDER QUEENS 1-7
By **Michael Gallon**

FOR THE LOVE OF BLOOD 1-4
By **Jamel Mitchell**

HOOD CONSIGLIERE 1&2
NO TIME FOR ERROR
By **Keese**

PROTÉGÉ OF A LEGEND 1,2&3
LOVE IN THE TRENCHES 1&2
By **Corey Robinson**

THE PLUG'S RUTHLESS DAUGHTER 1&2
By **Tony Daniels**

BORN IN THE GRAVE 1-3
CRIME PAYS
By **Self Made Tay**

MOAN IN MY MOUTH
By **XTASY**

TORN BETWEEN A GANGSTER AND A GENTLEMAN
By **J-BLUNT & Miss Kim**

LOYALTY IS EVERYTHING 1-3
CITY OF SMOKE 1-3
By **Molotti**

HERE TODAY GONE TOMORROW 1&2
By **Fly Rock**

WOMEN LIE MEN LIE 1-4
FIFTY SHADES OF SNOW 1-3
STACK BEFORE YOU SPLURGE
GIRLS FALL LIKE DOMINOES
NAÏVE TO THE STREETS
By **ROY MILLIGAN**

PILLOW PRINCESS
By **S. Hawkins**

SECURE DA BAG | IRA B.

THE BUTTERFLY MAFIA 1-3
SALUTE MY SAVAGERY 1&2
By **Fumiya Payne**

THE LANE 1&2
By Ken-Ken Spence

THE PUSSY TRAP 1-5
By **Nene Capri**

DIRTY DNA
By **Blaque**

SANCTIFIED AND HORNY
by **XTASY**

BOOKS BY LDP'S CEO, CA$H

TRUST IN NO MAN
TRUST IN NO MAN 2
TRUST IN NO MAN 3
BONDED BY BLOOD
SHORTY GOT A THUG
THUGS CRY
THUGS CRY 2
THUGS CRY 3
TRUST NO BITCH
TRUST NO BITCH 2
TRUST NO BITCH 3
TIL MY CASKET DROPS
RESTRAINING ORDER
RESTRAINING ORDER 2
IN LOVE WITH A CONVICT
LIFE OF A HOOD STAR
XMAS WITH AN ATL SHOOTER

www.ingramcontent.com/pod-product-compliance
Lightning Source LLC
LaVergne TN
LVHW010917110826
845149LV00013B/2403

* 9 7 8 1 9 7 1 7 7 0 1 0 9 *